JPB SUMMER READING LEE

Lee, Ingrid

Dog lost

FROM THE CHICKEN HOUSE

Not all Italians love pasta, and there's an occasional Jamaican citizen who hates reggae! So while being careful about all dogs we don't know, just as in humans, no one race, breed or colour should ever be judged by prejudice.

Here's a wonderful story that shows us why!

BARRY CUNNINGHAM,
Publisher.

Dog Lost

INGRID LEE

Chicken House

2 Palmer Street, Frome, Somerset BA11 1DS

For Susan, who loves all dogs

Text © Ingrid Lee 2008
First published in Great Britain in 2008
This edition published in 2010
The Chicken House
2 Palmer Street
Frome, Somerset BA11 1DS
United Kingdom
www.doublecluck.com

Cover design by Tracey Paris
Interior design by Steve Wells
Printed and bound in Great Britain by CPI Bookmarque, Croydon

3 5 7 9 10 8 6 4 2

British Library Cataloguing in Publication data available.

ISBN 978-1-906427-55-9

Council considering pit bull ban

28 February

Crickstead council is considering a region-wide ban on pit bull terriers. 'They are four-legged ticking time bombs,' Mayor Michael Dryden told *The Star*.

'If we are going to ban or restrict other dangerous weapons, we should include these animals as well,' Dryden said yesterday. 'It's our duty to protect our neighbourhoods.'

'Pit bulls are a major threat. Nobody would think of bringing a lion into a children's playground. In the same way, we have to ensure that the public are properly protected from these dangerous beasts.'

Pit bulls are not a specific breed. A pit bull is generally regarded as a cross between a bull breed of dog and larger dogs like the mastiff.

Cash hung out of a window. So did the boy. Cold air sucked the air from their lungs. It was snowing, and the boy clapped his hands at a fat flake. Cash tried to copy him, snapping the ice in her white puppy teeth. When the boy cooed at a pigeon hiding under the drainpipe, Cash stuck out her muzzle. Her chin trembled. Finally she blew out a little 'hyuh'.

Mackenzie laughed. He rubbed her head. 'Cash,' he said. 'You're a great bird-dog, Cash!'

Cash wriggled her bum. The boy smelled good – hot and salty. He talked to her.

'Cash. Come here, Cash. There's a good girl. I love you, Cash.'

ONE

Mackenzie lay under his covers in the dark. He counted each flat footstep slamming up the stairs.

One, two, three ... He pulled his pillow close and peered into the night.

Seven, eight, nine ... His bones locked.

Eleven, twelve ... The door swung open. Bright light from the hall invaded his room, and a dark figure walked up to the bed. 'Here,' a voice grunted. 'Tried to cash in my chips and ended up with this for my trouble. Mind you don't let it chew up my shoes.'

A wet lump landed on Mackenzie's bed. Seconds

later the door slammed shut. The bedroom was black again.

Mackenzie curled away from the damp weight that trembled on top of the blanket. He could feel hot air whistle past his ear. He could smell fear. And he could make out the splotches of white. When he found the courage to touch one of them, it crumpled in his hand like heavy silk.

It was an ear, a soft silky ear.

Something began to whack his leg. Mackenzie worked it out. A tail was beating against his leg. The prod in his tummy was a paw. And the cold dry poke under his neck, well, that was a nose.

The thing on his bed was a dog. A dog! His father had thrown a dog on the bed.

In the dark Mackenzie lay still, holding the ear lightly. Just as he was getting used to the soft way it folded in his fingers, the dog licked his chin, a slurpy ice-cream lick. Mackenzie slid his hand from the ear to the smooth damp head. He ran his hand on down the neck and curled his fingers into the loose skinny folds. He waited. After a bit the dog stopped trembling and settled into the covers like warm butter. It was going to sleep.

'Cash,' whispered Mackenzie. His father had called the dog Cash. Mackenzie closed his eyes and breathed carefully, breathing in with the dog, breathing out with the dog. He stayed as still as a sleeping boy.

It wasn't that long before he was a sleeping boy.

So that's how Mackenzie and Cash spent their first night together, wrapped up close, nose to nose. In the morning they got quite a surprise when they opened their eyes. Both of them jumped. They didn't know that the other was really there. They thought it was just a dream.

Mackenzie took a good look at the dog lying on his pillow. It yawned, so he got a good look inside and out. It had a long pink tongue and bright brown eyes. And it was a puppy, a girl puppy. Mackenzie was pretty certain about that.

The puppy looked back at Mackenzie. She saw a freckled nose. She looked right into Mackenzie's blue eyes with her big brown ones, and sneezed. She blew spit all over his face.

They both scrambled out of bed.

Mackenzie followed Cash down the stairs. The puppy was in so much of a hurry, her paws slipped on the bare wood and Mackenzie had to grab her tail to slow her down. He pushed her out into the back garden. It was early spring and still chilly, so they both shivered while the puppy did her business. She was as glad as Mackenzie was to get back into the house, especially when the morning train whistled shrilly beyond the fence.

Back in the middle of the kitchen, the puppy looked at Mackenzie and wagged her tail. Where was breakfast?

Mackenzie didn't know what puppies ate for breakfast. Whatever it was, he knew they didn't have it in the house. Finally he gave the puppy a bowl of bran flakes swimming in milk, and a piece of bread and peanut butter. She seemed to like that a lot.

With fifteen minutes to go before the school bus, Mackenzie and Cash climbed back upstairs. Cash didn't know that going up steps was just as tricky as going down. She slipped and knocked her noggin. Mackenzie picked her up and hauled her the rest of the way so she didn't come to any more harm. It was a tough job. The puppy wriggled, and bits and pieces of her kept slipping out of his grasp. It was like trying to hang on to a sack of rubber balls.

When they finally got to Mackenzie's bedroom, Mackenzie took a long look at his new dog. He had to go to school, and he wanted a picture to carry with him all day long. She looked good enough to eat. Her coat was a caramel colour, laced with brown sugar and milk. Next to her nose, where the hair was short, you could see her skin, pink as bubble gum. Mackenzie thought she was going to be a big dog, a beautiful big dog. But right then, she was just a pudding pot of puppy with a wet nose and a plump rump full of wriggles.

All the while Mackenzie was memorizing Cash, she was memorizing him. She must have liked the way he looked. Her tail wagged the whole time.

Anybody could see they were love-struck.

At the last minute Mackenzie remembered to leave Cash a drink. He filled his old fish bowl at the bathroom sink, letting the water run until it was ice cold. He put some newspapers in the corner too, just in case. Then he gave the puppy a hug and closed his door. 'I'll be back before you know it, Cash,' he called as he ran downstairs. 'We'll go out!'

Cash was asleep under the bedclothes before the school bus got to the end of the road. She hadn't felt so warm and safe for a long time, or so full either. She stuck her pink snout into the pillow, where it still smelled of the boy, and let her belly spread out wider than a jam doughnut.

At school, Mackenzie didn't have it as easy. But he did his best to make the day go by. He wrote a sum on the board and read a poem out loud. In between lessons he thought about Cash. 'I've got a dog,' he thought.

At lunch he cleaned the chalk ledge for his teacher and emptied the recycling bin. 'She's waiting for me,' he thought.

During the music lesson he kept time with the rhythm sticks. 'We'll go to the park,' he decided.

Mackenzie looked out of the window anxiously. The sun was shining. The sky was bluer than a robin's egg.

'I've got a dog named Cash,' he wrote in the corner of his notebook.

TWO

After the school bus dropped him off at home, Mackenzie was up the stairs in a flash. He flung open the door of his room and filled his arms with puppy.

'Rrrrrgh!' Cash cried. She tried to lick Mackenzie's face off. She squirmed so much that she plopped out of his grip. Mackenzie had to lie on the floor so she could sprawl over his chest and give him a proper hello.

When all the smooching was done, Mackenzie said, 'You need to go out.' He looked around the room and found an old belt. He cut off the end, then took the point of the scissors and dug them into the strap to make a hole. When he put it around Cash's neck, it was a bit loose. 'There,' he said. 'That's your collar. You'll grow into it.'

In the kitchen drawer there were some old metal clips. Mackenzie attached one of them to the belt buckle. Then he tied a bit of yellow rope to the clip and made a loop at the other end for holding. Some of his brother's old football tape helped to give it a grip. 'Come here, Cash,' he called to the puppy.

Cash thought that the rope was a toy. She grabbed hold of it and shook it between her teeth. She shook the rope so hard she addled her brains. Her snout smacked the side of the kitchen table. Ouch!

'No, Cash.' Mackenzie held her head steady in his hands. 'That's your lead,' he explained carefully. 'So you don't get lost. Now we're going out!'

As soon as Cash felt the spring sunshine, she took off. Mackenzie practically had to fly to keep up. The trouble was that Cash didn't know about straight lines. She only knew about circles. She ran around and around Mackenzie so many times that they got tied together like a birthday present.

A fat grey squirrel finally helped them get untangled.

It waved its bushy tail right under Cash's nose and the puppy raced after it with conviction, half dragging Mackenzie all the way down the street. When the squirrel scampered up a grand oak, Cash was so caught up in the chase, she forgot to stop. Pow! She bopped her nose. It was such a surprise, she fell back on her bum and howled.

'Poor Cash!' cried Mackenzie. He sat on the kerb and rubbed her head. He kissed her nose until the puppy was ready to run again.

They ran all the way to the park. A big black dog was walking its mistress up the path. As soon as it saw Cash, it started to bark, standing up on two legs and pawing the air.

Cash scuttled behind Mackenzie and shoved her head between his legs. 'Rrrrrgh!' she cried. She was brave up front, but her back end trembled. She tucked her tail out of sight.

'Down, Fedora, down!' the lady cried to her dog. She had to hold on to the lead with both hands. She looked at Cash's big head stuck between Mackenzie's knees. 'Young man,' she said to Mackenzie, 'that dog of yours should have a muzzle.' She pulled her big barky dog away. 'A dog like that has no business in a public park,' she huffed.

Mackenzie bent down. 'It's all right, Cash,' he soothed. 'You're a good dog. You'll be big like that dog someday. And twice as clever. Come on. I'm going to show you a rabbit hole.'

The rabbit hole had stretched a bit over the winter. No rabbits had lived there for a long time, but lots of dogs had scratched away at the sides. Mackenzie and Cash stuck their heads down the hole and sniffed. Mackenzie didn't smell anything, but Cash must have smelled a hot treat because she got excited – so excited she fell in. Mackenzie had to pull her out by the tail.

'Cash,' he laughed, 'you're a dog, not a sink plug. Come on! Let's go to the pond.'

Cash had never seen so much water all at once. She pranced back and forth through the rushes that lined the edges of the pond. She tried to get a drink and keep her feet dry at the same time. First she tried lifting one paw and leaning forwards. When that didn't work, she lifted the other paw and leaned sideways. Her tongue just wouldn't reach. After dancing back and forth like that for a minute, she gave up all the fancy stuff. She jumped in the pond headfirst and tried to drink it dry.

'Whoa, Cash!' whooped Mackenzie. He fished her out by the tail. They both got soaked. 'Good thing you've got a handle. Otherwise you'd be sucking up minnows from the bottom!'

It was getting late in the day. They sprawled out in the clover and let the last of the sun dry them off. Cash was asleep before Mackenzie had finished wringing out his socks. She was a puppy. She needed plenty of naps.

'Cash,' Mackenzie said quietly. He squirmed over sideways until he could talk into one of her ears. He rubbed her rump. 'Cash, I've got so much stuff to tell you. Good stuff and bad stuff.'

He started talking like there was no end to the words. 'I've got a mother, Cash. She's dead. You won't ever get to meet her. But I'll tell you about her anyway.'

A clover whiffled against Cash's nose. She turned her belly up so that Mackenzie could scratch it while he told his stories.

Mackenzie kept talking. 'Mum always smelled good. Sort of like soap and lemons. She used to come up to my room at night, before I went to sleep.

She never forgot. Sometimes she'd stay for a while and tell me a story. Her stories were good, especially the funny ones. One time she told me why toads burp. I'll tell you that story sometime, Cash. After you've seen a toad for yourself.'

Mackenzie flipped Cash's ears over so the insides could dry. Then he rolled over too and stared at the sky. He kept talking. 'Sometimes my mum would fall asleep right in the middle of a story. I always let her sleep, even though I wanted to hear the end. She could never stay long, 'cause after a bit my dad would yell up the stairs. Then she'd wake up and I knew she'd go. But she always blew wishes around my bed when she turned off the lights.'

Mackenzie raised himself on one elbow. 'My room is full of wishes. Mum said they stuck to things and that every once in a while, one would rub off and come true. That's what you are,' he said, looking at Cash. 'One of my wishes.'

The puppy sighed. She knew all about wishes.

Mackenzie wasn't quite finished. He reached over and grabbed a clover. He started to pluck the petals from it. 'My mum had some sort of disease. That's why she needed so much sleep. One morning she just never woke up. The last time I saw her she was sleeping in a bed of flowers – sort of like these ones. They were all around her. That time I couldn't help myself. I called for her out loud, Cash. But she was so tired, she didn't wake up. Even when I yelled as loud as I could.'

Mackenzie stopped talking and Cash opened her eyes. For a while the two of them watched the water in the pond.

'She was just the best,' Mackenzie said.

On the way home Mackenzie and Cash stopped on the street to look down a sewer. A lady opened her front door. 'Good Lord!' she exclaimed to Mackenzie. 'You got one of them fighting dogs. You keep him away from my property, do you hear? Or I'll have the police out.' She went back inside her house and slammed the door.

Cash stuck her tail between her back legs again. 'Never mind that, Cash,' Mackenzie said. 'You'll get used to it. The people around here are just the door-slamming kind.'

James O'Rourke was at the window when they got to the house. He stuck his head out of the front door and grunted to Mackenzie. 'That mutt looks wet. I don't want the house smelling like damp dog. It stays out till it's dry.'

Then he slammed the door.

THREE

It was dinner time. There was macaroni cheese on the table, and ketchup.

James O'Rourke took a slug of whisky and stared at his son. 'Where's that mutt?' he asked Mackenzie.

'She's in my room,' said Mackenzie. 'She's a great dog. Thanks, Dad.'

'Keep it away from the furniture,' O'Rourke grunted. 'And if I hear barking, there'll be trouble. I'm a working man. I need my sleep. Don't know how the woman talked me into keeping that thing.'

'The woman' was James O'Rourke's girlfriend. He had hooked up with her just about the time

Mackenzie's half-brother ran off. Her name was Jane. Jane had long black hair with a fringe that ended at eye level. The ends of it were so pointy, Mackenzie was surprised she didn't blind herself. Jane was fond of red lipstick too. When she talked, Mackenzie sometimes forgot to look at the rest of her. He just watched her red lips slide around in her face.

'Cash is a good dog,' said Mackenzie. He looked at the rest of the macaroni in the pot. There wasn't much left. Cash would be hungry too.

'It came with a bag of food,' his dad said. 'It's in the car.'

After dinner Mackenzie found the food. It was a big bag. He dragged it up the stairs and mixed a handful with the macaroni. The puppy ate as if tomorrow was next week. Mackenzie could see her tummy swelling like a party balloon. Afterwards they sat together in the corner of the bedroom. Cash rolled over and grabbed Mackenzie's trouser leg. She shook it in her teeth. She growled. She fell asleep with the cloth still in her mouth.

Mackenzie rubbed her swollen tummy. 'Cash,' he whispered, 'I haven't told you everything. We have a brother too. He's still alive. At least, I think he is.'

Mackenzie relaxed against the wall and thought about his brother. His name was Kid. He hadn't been gone that long, and Mackenzie remembered everything about him. Kid and Mackenzie had shared the room once and his bed was still there. It was the top bunk.

Kid was a lot older – almost eight years older. And he wasn't really his brother, he was a ... a half-brother. Mackenzie always thought that was funny. 'What's the other half?' he asked once.

Kid snorted. 'The other half's a monkey's uncle.'

For brothers, even half-brothers, they didn't look much alike. Mackenzie was pale and blond. Kid looked like he was varnished in teak oil. 'My mum was a gypsy moth,' Kid told Mackenzie. 'After she ran away, the old man caught a butterfly. Too bad she died on him.'

After he said that, Kid apologized. 'Sorry Mac, I know she was your mum. I liked her a lot too. It's just that ... well ... she wasn't *my* mother.'

'Where's your mother now?' Mackenzie asked.

Kid didn't like the question much. He always tried to change the subject. 'I don't know,' he said. 'She sent letters for a while. But then she just said she had to get on with her life. Come on, let's get some grub.'

Mackenzie remembered those nights his dad stayed out and Kid did the cooking. Kid was a good cook and his suppers were better than pizza – some rice and bacon with onions, or maybe cheese on toast with black pepper and pickle.

Afterwards, Kid usually went out. He said he had friends. He went out so much he must have had a friend for every night of the week. Often he got home late. If he ran into their dad, the two of them would start yelling at each other. They'd yell about Kid's night roaming. Or about the cost of a can of tuna. Or about the colour of the kitchen sink. They could always find something to yell about.

The yelling always woke Mackenzie up. He'd listen and wait.

By the time he got upstairs, Kid was always agitated. His breathing came quick and raspy.

Once Mackenzie said, 'You gotta be careful, Kid. He might do something bad to you.'

Kid never answered. Or else he said, 'Not your business, Mac.' The last time he added, 'Better if I just get out.'

The next morning Kid's bed was empty. Some of his clothes were gone, and so was Mackenzie's jar of coins. There was a note on the window.

Take care of yourself. I've got to get out. Sorry about the money. You can have my stuff. I'll write.
Kid

Of course he never did – write, that is.

Mackenzie opened his eyes. All that had happened three years ago, when he was only eight. Now he was eleven. Mackenzie looked up at the top bunk. He looked down at the sleeping puppy. Finally he started talking again. 'You don't need to know much about my brother, Cash. Kid's going to come back some day. Then you'll see him for real. You can have his old blanket till then. So you'll already know what he smells like. Maybe … maybe you'll find him first. Maybe you'll find him for me.'

The second night Mackenzie and Cash slept under Kid's blanket in the corner.

FOUR

Mackenzie lived at 269 Chester Street. It was a run-down street at the tired end of town. Railway tracks ran along the end of the garden, just like they did at the end of all the other gardens on the north side of the street. Beyond the tracks there was only the river, a lazy brown waterway smelling of old mud and rotting grass. Six times a day, a train trundled the narrow corridor between the properties and the river, bound to and from the city station.

The last night run was always the same. The train pulled away from the city centre at 11:03 sharp, crammed full of sports fans, theatre-goers and office cleaners heading home. Everyone grabbed a seat. Some talked. Some slept.

Except Abi Waters. The young woman always knelt on her seat and opened the slit window right at the top. She liked to press her face against the opening and take in the night air as it rushed by her face. It smelled of river stink, but Abi never noticed. Every breath was sweet to her.

Abi was thinner than a twig. Her cheeks were rosy, so she looked like she was blooming. But most of the time she was dying. That's why she went to the city. Three times a week, three o'clock sharp, she made the train trek all the way from her house in Rooksbury. Her kidneys were failing and she needed hospital treatment. By six o'clock she was stretched between stiff white sheets and doing her maths homework while a machine scrubbed her blood clean. Three times a week the eleven o'clock train took her back home.

The back gardens sailed by at a fair clip as Abi stared at the houses through the opening. Most of them weren't much to look at, even in the dark: worn-out slums, with dirty windows and peeling paint. Only the odd occupant had hung up cheerful curtains or put out a few plastic knick-knacks.

The scenery changed. Of course, the one side was always river, but the houses on the other side ended abruptly, and then the train rolled by a row of warehouse car parks. After that there was nothing but wide-open field. It stretched away from the tracks to the distant street lights, a sorry mess of broken concrete, plastic rubbish and weeds. That barren ground gave Abi the shivers, and she always turned away to watch the river instead. Only the old distillery wedged between the water and the tracks blocked her view for a brief few seconds.

A long time ago the distillery had been a busy place. The train had stopped there to unload grain for the big whisky vats, and the air was always full of the smell of malt. Now the place was condemned. Even the homeless were sent packing: the ground floor entrances were blocked with plywood, and a big sign screamed KEEP OUT!

Abi turned around just as the train came up to the back gardens of Chester Street, on the far side of the field. The first house belonged to an old lady. Her name was Mrs Brody and she was the only original homeowner left on the street. Abi Waters didn't know that. All she knew was that the old lady liked to stand at her bedroom window and watch the last train of the night flash past.

Tonight was the same as the other nights. The old lady in the window carefully raised her arm, silhouetted against her bedroom light. Abi waved back. Then she closed the window and sat down in her seat. It was 11:11. The train was right on schedule. She'd be home soon.

A minute later the train lumbered past Mackenzie's house. He and Cash watched it go by from their bedroom window too.

FIVE

PC Dean always began his afternoon shift with a drive down Chester Street. The houses there had seen tough times. Most of them were rented out, and the landlords didn't care that the gardens were weedy and the eaves stuffed full of leaves. The renters didn't seem to care either. They had bigger problems.

Dean drove down the street until it ended by the empty field. He turned his police car round and looked at the last house. One Chester Street. Mrs Brody's house.

Dean had a soft spot for old people, and he

judged that Mrs Brody was close to eighty. She lived alone and never went out. Meals-on-Wheels brought her dinner twice a week. As Dean pulled out of the turn, he spotted a volunteer in the driveway. She was carrying a large tray towards her old Jetta.

Dean rolled down his window.

'Afternoon, Miss Smithers,' he said. 'How's everything?'

Miss Smithers smiled at PC Dean, and her violet eyes blossomed. 'I brought Mrs Brody a hot chicken dinner,' she said. 'Most of the time she eats nothing but cold food out of tins.'

PC Dean shook his head. 'It's a strange world,' he said. 'Mrs Brody still owns the house. A place by the river is worth money, run-down or not. She could sell out and live comfortably somewhere in an old people's home. Here, she's got no one to keep an eye on her.'

Miss Smithers looked at PC Dean, and he looked back at her. Remarkable eyes, he thought. Colour like lilac blooms or crocuses, or some such flower.

Miss Smithers put the empty tray in her car boot. 'Mrs Brody's got more people keeping an eye on her than some folk,' she said. 'Right now she's got you.

And she's got me.' She got into her car and waved goodbye. She still had two more stops to make, and the food wouldn't stay hot for ever.

PC Dean followed her to the next corner and got on with his beat. There were lots of other streets to cover, and the people working late along the development road needed to know he was out there.

At the end of his shift he drove down Chester Street one more time. He caught a glimpse of the night train at the edge of the dark field. It was Tuesday, and the girl with the pale, flyaway hair pressed herself against the tiny open window at the back, waving at something or other.

PC Dean checked his watch. 11:11 p.m., the same as always. The train was so regular you could set your watch by it. Dean headed back to the station.

Four houses down the street, in a cold back shed, two dogs licked at their paws. They shifted about, trying to escape the weight of their chains. They eyed the food left just outside their cages. One of them would get it. The other one wouldn't. The dogs hated each other because of that.

The only other things in the shed were a treadmill and some bits of fur.

SIX

Mackenzie and Cash got along like a house on fire. Whenever Mackenzie went out, Cash waited in the bedroom. There was always water and food, and Kid's blanket. And Cash had a teddy too. She worried that bear every day. She pulled at the stuffing until it looked as if someone had let out all the air. Flat teddy. She ate the button eyes.

After school Mackenzie blew in through the bedroom door like the answer to a prayer. He said the same thing he always did: 'Come on, Cash! It's time to go out!'

The outdoors was their big playground. There

were so many things to do: fetch a stick, roll in the grass, check out a hole. And they always ran to the tree with the squirrel's nest. Cash learned how to skid to a stop just in time so that her nose was safe.

One day Cash didn't stop running when she got to the tree. She just kept right on going. She climbed until she was way over Mackenzie's head. And when she came back down, she landed lightly on all four legs. After that, Cash tried to climb that tree every time. She could make it right up to the first branch, no problem. The grey squirrel took to a higher lookout.

One day Cash scrabbled up so high that Mackenzie had to let the lead go, so the dog wouldn't choke. 'Good girl, Cash,' said Mackenzie. 'Some day you'll make it right to the top.'

Cash grew and grew. The bag of puppy food disappeared. 'Cash needs more food,' Mackenzie told his father. 'She's a big dog now.'

His father said, 'Don't bother me with that.'

Mackenzie said, 'She's got to eat.'

His father went upstairs and slammed his door.

That night Cash had cereal. She had cereal the next day too. The day after that there was a bag of food on the doorstep. As Mackenzie dragged it up to his room, his father complained. 'Nobody told me that dog was going to get so big. I'm not made of money.'

Summer slipped away in a blaze of heat. Mackenzie and Cash spent a lot of time at the park, their feet in the pond. They stayed away from people. Everyone had too much to say.

'You got a permit for that dog, boy? I'm going to report that dog.'

'Dogs like that ought to be banned. People have a right to feel safe.'

'You boys are all the same. You think a vicious dog makes you look tough.'

At the park Cash got to know all the animals. She knew what rabbits smelled like. She learned how high frogs could jump. And she could catch flies. When Mackenzie went back to school, she napped. You could see her ears move and her lips twitch. She was back at the park in her dreams.

The days got colder. One day it started to snow. The snow turned the world into a freshly-plumped pillow. Mackenzie and Cash ate their supper in a big hurry, then went out. Mackenzie jumped into a drift and came up with a treasure stuck to his glove – a pine cone. He threw the cone into the air.

Cash watched the cone nose-dive back into the snow. She pounced on the puncture in the smooth surface and dug and snuffled and sneezed, till she was right down in the white stuff. Only her rear end stuck out, her tail wagging hard enough to bat tennis balls. When she came up for air, she had the cone in her chops. Snow stuck to her whiskers and lashes and the hair inside her ears. It sat like a hat on her head. She looked like a snow dog.

'Hooray, Cash! Good for you!' Mackenzie cheered. 'That's a good dog! Come on!'

They zigzagged down the street as the street lights popped on. The snowy banks along the road got more rumpling than bed sheets. Afterwards, the boy and the dog eased in through the door and sneaked back up the stairs. Safe in their cosy room, they rolled into their blankets and fell straight to sleep. The night was full of soggy snores.

The next night they built a snowman in the back garden. Cash tried to carry its head in her mouth. Mackenzie laughed. He dug the pine cone out of his pocket. 'Here Cash, catch this.'

After Cash had chewed the pine cone to bits, Mackenzie used the seeds to give the snowman a big grin and a pair of eyes. 'It can watch the night train,' said Mackenzie.

When they got back inside, Mackenzie told Cash to sit while he fetched a rag to rub her dry. But the dog couldn't stop herself from shaking. Water splashed on to the wall. Mackenzie's father came down the stairs at the same time, ready for a night on the town with his fancy lady friend. Some of the melted snow freckled his trouser leg.

It never took much for James O'Rourke to lose his temper. *Whack!* He planted his black shiny shoe right into Cash's soft belly.

Cash hit the wall. She yelped. She stuck her tail under her bum. She cried.

Mackenzie grabbed her. 'Sorry, Dad. She's a good dog. She's sorry. She won't do that again.'

'That dog's getting too big for this house. It'd better not have ruined these trousers!' yelled his father. He slammed out of the door.

Cash crept up to their room. She crawled on to her blanket and cried like a baby. Mackenzie followed her. He sat on the floor and put his arms around her.

'You're a good dog, Cash,' he whispered. 'But you've got to be careful. You've got to stay out of his way.'

Cash hung her head. She licked the sore spot on her tummy. She put her big head in the boy's lap and stared at the wall.

'I'll take care of you, Cash,' said Mackenzie. 'I promise. You've just got to stay out of his way.'

The winter passed and spring chased the snow away. Cash was careful. She stayed in Mackenzie's room when Mackenzie went to school. Sometimes she put her paws on the window and watched for the school bus. Sometimes she chewed on a pine cone.

Mackenzie didn't like leaving her at home, but he took good care of her, just as he had promised. Until one day he couldn't.

SEVEN

Mackenzie sat on the floor and leaned against his bed. 'Paw, Cash. Come on, there's a good girl. Give me your paw.' He lifted his puppy's paw, the brown one, and gave it a little shake. It slipped back to the floor.

'Come on, Cash. Paw!' He repeated his actions again and again. Finally Cash responded. She lifted her paw slowly, like it was heavy.

'Yeah!' Mackenzie cheered, giving the paw a good shake. 'That's your paw, Cash! You're a clever dog.' He gave her a hug.

Cash wagged her tail and lifted her paw in the air

again. She lifted it so high Mackenzie had to shake it one more time. He had to give her a kiss.

After that Cash didn't stop. She sat waving her paw back and forth like she was in a parade.

Mackenzie went to his desk. Miss Smithers had set them some geography questions to answer for homework. 'That's all for now, Cash,' he said. 'I've got homework to finish. You can play with your toy.'

Cash put her ears down. She went into the corner and chewed on her teddy. Mackenzie got to the third question and looked up. 'Hey, Cash,' he said. 'Still got that paw?'

Cash stayed in her corner. She studied her tail. She acted as if Mackenzie wasn't even there. So he went back to his homework. *The upward pressure of magma causes the earth to fold or crack into ...* He became so preoccupied that he didn't see Cash come out of her corner. The dog put her teddy in Mackenzie's lap. She waved her paw in the air.

'Awwwww, Cash,' Mackenzie said. He read the next question. *'What type of mountain is formed when magma forces its way through a weakness in the earth's crust?'*

Cash pushed the book away with her nose, and

held up her paw higher than ever.

Mackenzie laughed. He put his pencil in the book to mark his place. 'OK, Cash. You win. Let's go out!'

It was a beautiful spring evening, the kind of day that jump-starts green growing things. Cash hurried after Mackenzie so fast that she missed a step and rolled all the way to the bottom of the stairs in a muddle of feet and tail and tummy. Mackenzie's dad was just coming through the door. He was angry. He had gone to Jane's house with pizza and whisky. But she was getting ready to go out with her girlfriends. She already had a new coat of red on her lips. She told him to go home.

Cash crashed right into him. The pizza slipped out of the box and splattered over the floor.

O'Rourke flared up. 'You stupid animal!' he yelled. He jabbed his boot hard into her ribs. His bottle of whisky hit the stair post and shattered, the glass bits showering the pizza slices with a glittery topping.

Cash landed on her belly and stuck her tail under her bum. She huddled against the doorjamb. Mackenzie went to grab her, but his father was already into another kick. His boot caught Mackenzie on the hip and sent him hard against the door.

Then Cash forgot to be scared. Her tail whipped up. She scrambled to her feet and planted herself in front of Mackenzie. Her shoulder blades bristled. She peeled back her lips and bared her teeth. She looked at O'Rourke with eyes as bright as candle flames.

She tried to growl.

That really was the last straw for James O'Rourke. He kicked at the pizza lying across the bottom stair. 'Dammit, you dog!' he cursed. 'You think you can snarl at me? You're toast.' He grabbed the puppy by the collar and hauled her out through the back door. The broken glass crunched under his feet.

Mackenzie tried to stop his dad. 'No, Dad!' he yelled. 'No. No!'

Cash shut up. She knew what 'no' meant. She listened to Mackenzie. She let herself be hauled away by the neck. She was such a good dog.

O'Rourke threw her in the boot of the car and slammed the lid.

'No!' Mackenzie screamed again. He ran after his dad and pleaded for his puppy. 'She didn't mean it. She was scared, that's all. She won't do it again. I'll tell her. She'll listen to me.' He pulled at his father's arm.

O'Rourke was in too much of a rage to listen. Nothing went right. 'Damned dog!' he ranted. 'No dog's going to threaten me in my own home – or anywhere else. I should've known better. Damn thing will be biting my arm off next.' He wrenched open the car door and got behind the steering wheel.

The car screeched out of the driveway.

'No, Dad. Please. Don't take her!' Mackenzie cried. 'Please. Daddy!' He ran after the old car as it headed down the street. He begged. He cried. He yelled. 'Cash! Cash!'

Mackenzie's father never even slowed down. And finally Mackenzie had no breath left. The car disappeared.

That was the time when Mackenzie couldn't keep his promise. He lost Cash. She wasn't even a year old. And she was the runt of the litter. She needed more time to grow up.

Now she was gone.

The neighbours closed their doors to all the commotion. It was just a family argument, that was all. And none of their business, that was for certain. They talked about it later, though, over the back fences.

Just like they always did.

When Mackenzie's mother had died, some of the neighbours had wiped away a tear or two. 'Gentle soul,' they said. 'Never had a harsh word for anyone.'

When Kid ran away, they shook their heads. 'That boy doesn't appreciate anything. Stays out all night. Heading for trouble.'

And when Mackenzie's dad took Cash away, they downright applauded. 'Can't trust those pit bulls. A menace to society,' they said. 'There's one dad who's finally found some sense.'

EIGHT

The boot of the car smelled of old oil and stale beer. Cash cowered behind the spare tyre. She was scared, scared by the noise of the engine and the lurching of the car. After the dark of the boot, the glare of the street lights blinded her.

James O'Rourke was still in a rage. He swung Cash out of the car. The collar snapped in his hand. When the dog squatted on the ground in front of a tyre, he kicked at her. 'Get out of here,' he yelled. 'Before I really lose my temper!' He swiped at her again.

Cash took off. She headed into the dark, scrambling away from the man, away from the bright street. By the time she stopped, she was in the middle of nowhere, in a wide field full of rubble. Rough dark shapes poked out of the ground and Cash picked her way between them. Finally she came to an orange tarpaulin stretched into a makeshift tent between a tangle of brick and wood. She crawled inside.

The boy would come for her.

She waited till morning. Then she waited all day. She never doubted. Mackenzie would come for her.

Cash stayed under the tarpaulin for two nights. It rained, and sometimes she stuck out her head to drink. But there was nothing to fill her belly. Her tummy skin sagged. The first mosquitoes hatched in the scummy pools caught in the plastic. They fed feverishly on Cash's tender ears and teats.

The second night she whimpered. She shook. She waited.

By then she knew the boy wasn't coming. She crawled out from under the tarpaulin. A small avalanche of water cooled the hot welts on her ears. She shook off the water and looked about her. She sniffed the damp night. Cautiously she lifted one paw over a pile of rubble.

'Yip!' The edge of an old tin lid sliced her paw. Cash backed up. She backed right under the tarpaulin and stayed put.

Another day passed.

On the third night Cash stuck up her nose and took a long sniff. She was starving, and somewhere between the stink of old cement and mossy slime, she could smell food. Timidly she ventured out again. She put her best paw forward – her shaking paw, the one that grabbed hugs. This time she checked the feel of the earth before shifting her weight. It felt all right. Again and again she lifted each foot up and put it down carefully. She picked her way through the debris as if she was walking on eggshells. The promise of food pulled her towards the street lights.

The food was inside paper. Cash knew paper. Sometimes Mackenzie brought her a treat wrapped in paper, and she had learned how to shake it loose with her baby teeth until the prize fell out. It was a game they had shared.

Not now. Now she tore at the bag. The paper was soaked in juice, so she ate some of that first. Then she came to the food: cold chips, a bun soaked in ketchup and some pickle. She ate every scrap and looked around for more. And there was more! Lots more. Mostly old chips, but there was also a bone and some soup still sealed in a container. By the time Cash had worn away the plastic coating, her gums were sore. But she still managed to lap up the soup.

She went back to the tarpaulin with the carton in her teeth, stopping only to catch a drink of water that had pooled in an old cement block. Her belly was full. She slept. She dreamed of Mackenzie's room and her teddy. She nosed the soup container in her sleep and imagined it was the boy.

Hot salty boy.

NINE

Miss Smithers was teaching a geography lesson. Her lavender glance slid over the class. 'Mackenzie,' she chided. 'You haven't heard a word I'm saying.'

Mackenzie fought down a wave of panic. Miss Smithers was no fool. He waited mutely for her to reach over and look at his notes, to look at all the blank lines, the rows of missing answers. He waited for the axe to fall.

Only it didn't. Miss Smithers took another look at him and stopped. Turning back to the class, she went on with the lesson. 'Over time, running water wears away the surrounding rock. When a river empties into a bigger body of water, it often leaves behind this sediment. That's how …'

Mackenzie let his teacher's voice drift into the background. The memory of the previous night filled his thoughts. There was no room left for fancy landscaping. He went over it again – and again.

After his father had torn out of the driveway, he had cleaned up the pizza and broken glass. He went back to his room, tidied Cash's bed and put new water in the fish bowl. Then he stood at the window and waited until the stars came out. He waited for his father to bring Cash home.

Only it didn't happen that way.

His father came back well after dark, smelling of beer and soy sauce. He plunked a carton of noodles on to the table. They were beef and ginger, Mackenzie's favourite.

When he looked at the food, Mackenzie thought he might be sick. 'Where's Cash?' he said. 'What did you do with her?'

'I gave that mutt away,' his father said. 'It's nothing but trouble. Costs too much to feed, and now the council wants me to buy a muzzle and get it micro-chipped. I've got better things to do with my money.'

'You gave her to me,' said Mackenzie.

'Look,' said his father. 'You listen here. With a dog like that, it's only a matter of time before she turns on you. A dog like that could tear you up. Then I'd have to take you to hospital for some fancy needle-work.'

Mackenzie said, 'She's my dog. She's still a baby.' He stood glaring at his father, his hands clenched into white fists. He could feel hot tears stinging his eyes.

His father ran out of excuses. He slammed his fist on the table, sending the noodles in all directions. 'I make the decisions in this house,' he shouted. 'And that dog's gone for good.'

'Mackenzie!' Miss Smithers' voice broke into Mackenzie's thoughts. She was close to losing her cool. 'What *has* come over you today? Don't you want to know how our earth reinvents itself?'

She took another look at Mackenzie and gave up. He doesn't even hear me, she thought. And whatever he's thinking about, it isn't water and rocks.

At lunchtime Miss Smithers discussed Mackenzie with some of the other teachers in the staff room.

'He seems tired,' she said. 'Maybe I should call his dad.'

Mr Dawson, the Year 5 teacher, shook his head. 'Not much use in that,' he said. 'Mackenzie's father has a chip on his shoulder. He'll listen to you for about ten seconds. Then he'll just blame you for not making his son pay attention. The guy fell apart after his wife died. By the look of it, I'd say he was hitting the bottle. When Mackenzie was in my class, some days I had to make sure the boy had lunch.' Mr Dawson took a bite of his sandwich and chewed thoughtfully. 'Actually, Mackenzie coped pretty well. There was a brother there that looked out for him.'

Miss Smithers frowned. 'I haven't seen any brother.'

Mrs Blake, the secretary, took a sip of her tea. 'The brother took off. Sometimes he used to come to the school and walk home with Mackenzie. A good-looking older boy. I think his name was Kid. When he stopped coming, I asked Mackenzie why. Mackenzie just said he had moved out.'

Mr Dawson looked more thoughtful. 'Actually, last spring Mackenzie changed a lot. By the end of the year he was quite cheerful. Always had his hand up, and kept my board clean for me. His marks went up too. I think he'd got a dog.'

Miss Smithers nodded in agreement. 'Mackenzie usually does his best. I've never known him not to do his homework, and yet today he wasn't even paying attention. Something's happened. I'll have to go easy on him and see if I can make out what's gone so wrong all of a sudden.' She took a forkful of her salad, thinking so hard that it could have been shredded paper for all she noticed. 'I'll ask him about his dog,' she decided. 'Maybe that will get him talking.'

Mackenzie hung out with his friends at lunchtime. Nobody really noticed that he wasn't joining in their games. Nobody noticed that he didn't have any lunch. They didn't notice his tired red eyes either. It was allergy season, and half the class looked worse than he did.

Mackenzie tried not to think of Cash. He tried not to think of his puppy any more. He didn't want to think of her in a strange place. He didn't want to think about her at all. It hurt too much. So he tried to think about nothing.

By the afternoon the effort had tired him out. He

felt his legs and arms become stiff, and his eyelids grow heavy. By the time Miss Smithers got to the art lesson, he was asleep sitting up in his chair, like a wilted pea plant. The other kids giggled, but Miss Smithers left him alone.

At the end of the day she stopped him by the coat rack and put her hand on his shoulder. 'Go to bed early, Mackenzie. Tomorrow is a new day.'

What would *she* know?

But he should have given her more credit.

That night Miss Smithers gave James O'Rourke a phone call. 'Just to let you know that Mackenzie's a good boy,' she said.

But O'Rourke knew she was fishing – he could just tell. At the end of the conversation Miss Smithers said, 'And of course he's so fond of his dog.'

O'Rourke put a stop to that kind of talk right away. 'I got rid of the damned thing,' he told her. 'It was a pit bull terrier. The whole street's afraid of it. I can't put the boy at risk, either. The council's going to ban them. That dog was just a lawsuit waiting to happen. I'm not made of money.'

'Oh,' said Miss Smithers. 'It's gone to an animal shelter, then?'

'Had it put down,' O'Rourke lied. 'Only decent thing to do with a dog nobody wants.'

TEN

Over the next three nights Cash learned about rubbish bins. She got to know where the pickings were good. She could slip out a bit of meat without hooking a scrap of the wrapping. And she was always careful to stay in the shadows and away from night owls out for a stroll or a snack.

But on the fourth night Cash went hungry. It was bin day. Cash didn't know about such things. She didn't know that the bin men came every Tuesday at three o'clock and hauled away the rubbish from a week of city living. By the time night rolled around and Cash started hunting, all her favourite spots were empty of food.

She roamed further down the street until she came across a beggar in a doorway.

The beggar swung at her. 'Get out, dog!' he hissed. 'This is my corner.'

Cash fled back to her shelter. It wasn't until she was hidden under the tarpaulin that she tried out her growl. Anyone standing within ten feet would have heard her practising. The low rumbles made the canvas rattle. All the puppy overtones were gone.

Meanwhile, James O'Rourke was making up with his girlfriend at a pub down the street. 'Aw,' said Jane. She snuggled up to her old man. 'You didn't really give away the dog, did you? I liked it. Your kid and that dog were mates. You're such a meanie.'

O'Rourke was pretty drunk. 'Baby, you want that dog, I'll get it for you,' he bragged. 'It's probably sitting right where I ditched it.'

He left Jane in the pub with a fresh drink and went out to make good his word. It was a chance to impress her, after all. When he got to the field, he waded into the weed and rubble. Once he was past the City Development notice, he headed towards the river, kicking tin cans and plastic fencing out of his way. 'Cash, you mongrel!' he yelled. 'Come here!'

Cash heard O'Rourke. She stood under the tarpaulin. Her ears went down. Her tail swung up. The muscles in her chest grew tight. She growled inside her head.

In her head that growl was deeper than thunder. But outside, it made no noise at all.

James O'Rourke walked right up to the tarpaulin. He stopped and lit a cigarette as Cash stood inside the tent growling to herself.

'Cash!' yelled O'Rourke. He flicked the cigarette butt away in disgust. It landed next to the orange plastic.

Cash watched the smoke swirl past her nose. The red tip of the cigarette was reflected in her eyes.

But it was as if she was turned to stone.

O'Rourke swore out loud. That dog was long gone. Probably run over by now, he guessed. Or in some animal shelter.

When he got back to the pub, he had a row with his girlfriend. She said that if he loved her, he would get another dog. He said that if she loved him, she'd move in. She said she wasn't taking care of no kid.

O'Rourke shut up. Even he couldn't blame Jane

for thinking that way. Mackenzie was getting a mind of his own. He was probably going to be hell to live with in a year or two. Just like the first one.

'Come on, baby,' O'Rourke wheedled, trying another tack. 'Give your old man a break. I'll get you a kitten. How'd you like that? Something to match those blue ice-chip eyes of yours.'

Jane leaned over and planted a red smacker on O'Rourke's cheek. 'Ooh,' she said. 'You're so sweet.'

Cash left the tarpaulin. She stepped on the cigarette butt. It was still hot though her paws were tougher now, already healed over more than once. She was hungry, but that could wait. She headed away from the street, towards the river. It was time to check out the old building way back on the far side of the tracks.

It was time to move.

She circled the building, nosing at the plywood nailed over the doors. Around the back, close to the river, she finally found what she was looking for – a way in. It was an old flap tunnel. With a bit of shoving, she wedged herself between the plywood slats and padded up the ramp. The incline emptied on to a metal walkway strung six metres above a cellar. The air smelled like Mackenzie's dad when he'd had too much to drink. There were more stairs at the other end.

Cash crossed the walkway confidently. She was an expert on stairs.

The main floor was a maze of draughty corridors lined with open doorways. There were body smells here, but they were old smells, long gone. She was alone.

Most of the rooms were empty, but one had a couple of old mattresses piled up in the corner. There were newspapers too, and some stained blankets. The window was still in one piece and the room was full of dusty moonlight. Cash stood at the doorway and took a long look. Compared to an orange tarpaulin stretched between some cement blocks, the room looked like heaven.

That night she sprawled over one of the old mattresses and dreamed again. She dreamed of the smell of laughter, and she dreamed of chasing a bee in the wind. Every once in a while she sighed. Her ears went up. Her nose hunted for a boy.

But no dog has a nose that good. Not even a pit bull.

ELEVEN

'A controversial bylaw to ban pit bulls was introduced to a city council on Tuesday, and now requires only final approval before becoming law. The proposed bylaw in Crickstead has attracted nationwide attention as more local governments consider adopting similar restrictions against selected breeds ...'

Mackenzie watched the news after school. It was added misery. He closed his eyes tight to keep in the tears. Tears were a waste of time. He went upstairs and opened his geography book. He had five oceans to memorize.

More salt water.

Late that night there was a discussion programme on the television. People were invited to phone in and have their say about the proposed pit bull bylaw.

Felicity of Greenborough called the ban a knee-jerk reaction. 'Pit bulls make wonderful pets,' she argued. 'All those dogs want to do is please their masters.'

Sheri of Titchville thought that the council was just looking for easy votes. 'It's not the dogs,' she insisted. 'It's the owners. Some people teach their dogs to scare others. People like that are losers.'

John Smith of Bridgetown agreed. 'Ban the owners,' he snorted. 'Keep the dogs.'

One caller wanted to know more about the breed. 'I can't work out just what a pit bull is,' he complained in an old, quavery voice. 'Everyone tells me something different.'

Some photos of pit bulls appeared on the screen. All the dogs looked different. They were different in shape, different in size and even different in colour.

'Those pictures don't help me,' declared the caller. 'You know what I think? I think you news people are as mixed up as I am. In World War 1, I served with dogs that looked like the ones in those pictures. Most of them were heroes.'

He hung up.

The presenter of the programme asked a member of the Dog Breeders' Association to describe the breed. 'Well,' said the breeder. 'It's no wonder people are confused. Crickstead Council says that a pit bull is a cross between a bull terrier type and a larger dog like a mastiff, or it can even be any dog that looks or acts like a pit bull.'

Next the television host showed an interview with a police official. 'My officers have encountered a number of dangerous situations involving pit bulls,' said the Chief Inspector. 'This proposed ban will help my officers, and police services across the city, to keep our community safe from dangerous dogs.'

A vet called in to object. 'Breed bans just don't work,' he argued. 'If you remove the so-called "pit bulls" from the city, people who want to own a vicious dog will simply turn to another breed.'

An agent of the RSPCA read the society's official statement: 'We believe that pit bulls which are bred responsibly, trained and provided with loving environments make wonderful pets. A pit bull puppy is no different from any other kind of puppy.'

Mackenzie could have told anyone that. Too bad he was asleep under a blue blanket full of puppy hair.

The final call of the evening was from a woman. She sounded upset. 'It's about time the council had all those monsters put down! The man next door has two pit bulls,' she said. 'They bark all day long. I've got a toddler and I'm scared one day those dogs will get out and hurt my baby. It's just not right, being scared in your own garden.'

At the end of the show the host thanked everyone for their participation. He was pretty happy with his night's work. The pit bull debate was good for his ratings.

On his way home from work, James O'Rourke stopped at a local pub. He downed his drink and pointed to the TV over the counter. 'My kid had one of those dogs,' he said to the barman. 'One day it practically tore off my leg. Good riddance, I say.'

The barman kept his mouth shut, but he didn't agree with O'Rourke. The way the barman saw it, no one was giving those dogs a fair chance.

Maybe he'd get a dog. Maybe he'd check out the animal shelters in the morning.

TWELVE

That summer Cash finished growing. She knew every rubbish bin along the street. She knew which ones would be overflowing by the end of the day. She knew which would contain mostly paper and chips, and which would have rib bones and rice. She knew the days on which the pickings were slim, and those on which she could get her fill. Most importantly, she knew which ones were away from the street lights.

Of course people saw her. One or two even phoned the RSPCA. With her white patches, she was an easy target. But there weren't many who spotted her more than once. Cash had a routine to avoid detection. It was to have no routine.

'Just hysteria,' said one of the dog wardens after they had checked out the train tracks behind the warehouses. 'People think they see a pit bull when it's only a fox on the prowl. It's just scaremongering by the papers.'

'Won't bc long before the ban is in force,' said his partner. 'That should put an end to the fuss.'

Cash's best hunting was at the end of the field where a long row of ramshackle shops and eateries lined both sides of the street. Usually she waited until the street was empty before she checked out the bins. But this time Darren McGuire stood lounging against a street lamp outside the burger bar, his trousers hanging so low the crotch was almost touching the pavement.

'Well, take a look at that,' he said to his two hangers-on. 'That's a pit bull nosing around the rubbish. No owner in sight. And it's got no collar. You'd better watch out, boys. That dog might think you're meat pies.'

The other two stared at the dog. 'It's not that big,' one of them said.

'Stuffy,' laughed Darren, 'what would you know? You're a runny-nosed punk with snot for sense.'

Stuffy sniffed. 'I thought they were supposed to be scary. That one looks like an overgrown lap dog.'

Darren took a closer look at the dog. 'It's just a runt,' he said. 'Not very old I'd guess. Maybe just a year or two. I wonder what it's doing down here all by itself.'

Darren had considered himself a bit of an expert on pit bulls ever since he started sponging off his uncle at 9 Chester Street. His uncle kept pit bulls in the cement shed at the back of the garden, usually two at a time. He kept them for fighting. The dogs were chained to posts and locked into cages. They got lots of exercise, though: every one of them was tied to the treadmill twice a day.

Darren smirked when he thought of the dogs. Once, one of them just couldn't keep running. By the time someone came to turn off the machine, every scrap of hair on its belly had been scraped off. That dog learned to run like crazy.

Jake piped up. 'I heard those dogs have got jaws of steel. Once they get their teeth into you, they hang on for grim death.'

At that Darren started to laugh again, a high shrill laugh. 'That's right, Jake. Like a miser and his money.'

But then Darren started thinking. You could almost see the wheels turning in his brain. He squinted into the yellow light around the bin, watching the dog circle it methodically. She had dark brown eyes, one buried in a patch of brown, the other floating on milk. Her muzzle showed a trace of pink. Her body was a patchwork of white and brindle. White legs and a tail that curved up. And withers so thin you could almost put your hands around them.

Cash looked up. The muscles in her chest tightened.

Darren whistled under his breath. 'Wheee-ew. A dog like that'd be worth money in the ring.' He'd struck gold.

Cash vanished before the words were out of his mouth. But Darren leaned back against the street lamp cheerfully. 'My boys,' he said, 'we're going to have to check out that dog. It'll come back. And we'll be here waiting. Maybe I'll buy it a burger.'

Stuffy and Jake were surprised. Darren wasn't

much of an animal lover. He was the kind of guy that threw crumbs at the birds before air pistol practice.

'You boys heading home? It's after midnight.' PC Dean rolled down the window of his car and stuck his head out.

Stuffy and Jake jumped.

'Yes sir,' they muttered. They started off down the street. But Darren went on lounging against the street lamp for a bit, just to make a point. It was a good ten seconds before he slouched after them.

PC Dean watched them go. He was used to rounding up strays. His car rolled a few more metres to the edge of the empty stretch of field. 'What a wasteland,' he muttered. 'Nothing but a trap for every bit of wandering rubbish.'

He could just make out the old distillery silhouetted against the tinsel of the night. Someone will get hurt in there one of these days, Dean thought. Probably a child. That's what it would take before the council coughed up decent money to restore the historic site.

The developers were dragging their heels too. They didn't like the fact that the development agreement ordered them to throw a park and a community centre into their big scheme. Dean grimaced at the sign planted a few yards from the street. It had a shiny fluorescent light over it. The light was out, but he could still read the bold words.

Clover Cup Park
A Residential and Commercial Community
For the Future
Todmorton Development Company
'Live, Work and Play in the City'

A faint movement deep in the field drew his attention away from the words. Some white shapes floated through the darkness.

Dean sighed. It was probably just plastic. But then again … maybe he'd hike out to the distillery one night and check on things. Just to make sure that none of the street kids had decided to set up house.

Just in case.

Dean never let things go. No wonder the other coppers called him a pit bull.

THIRTEEN

Spring turned to summer in a blur. Mackenzie looked for Cash. He went to the park every day, all summer long, hoping to see her with her nose stuck in a rabbit hole. The lady with the black dog was there. The dog always barked at him.

His dad said he'd given her away, but Mackenzie didn't believe that for a minute. One day he had even phoned the RSPCA.

'RSPCA Animal Centre,' the voice at the other end answered.

'I'm looking for my dog,' said Mackenzie. 'She's … she's run away.'

'Does she have a collar and tag?' the voice asked.

'Uh … no, I just got her. We didn't have time to—'

The voice interrupted. 'There's a fine for not having a collar and tag.'

Mackenzie tried again. 'I just want to know if you've got her.'

The voice sounded exasperated. It was an 'OK, you sound like you're just a kid and I'm sorry to hear about your dog, I like animals too,' kind of voice. 'Just a minute.'

After a few moments another voice came on the line. 'Can I help you?'

'I lost my dog,' repeated Mackenzie. 'I just want to know if she's there.'

'I need to know her breed, age and any special markings,' the voice replied.

'She's a pit bull. She's about a year old. She's got a white coat with brown patches and a long tail and a pink nose.'

'Son.' The voice sounded tired now. It sounded like the first voice. 'Most of the dogs here are pit bulls, and they're all young. None of them is more than three years old. Most don't make it any longer than that. Maybe you should come down and look at the dogs for yourself.'

So Mackenzie went to the RSPCA centre. He took three buses and finally he found the building, a run-down place covered in city soot. The inside was friendlier. There were posters of animals plastered on the wall, and there was a big fish tank.

'Hello,' said the girl behind the desk. She was wearing blue overalls.

'I want to see the dogs,' said Mackenzie. 'My dog is missing.'

'Through those doors,' the girl nodded. She didn't ask him if his dog had a collar and tag. She could tell right away what the answer would be. She just said, 'Every dog that leaves here from now on has to be micro-chipped with the new owner's address, and have proof of vaccination. The package is ninety quid.'

Mackenzie didn't know what to say.

'Well, you can at least look and see if it's there,' she went on. 'I've got to tell you that, that's all. It'd cost me my job if I didn't.'

Inside there were four rows of cement cages with bars across the front. Some of the dogs were barking. Mackenzie walked down the rows. The voice on the phone was right, there was a pit bull in most of the cages. There were chocolate-brown ones with pink noses, brindled ones with pink noses and two that had markings just like Cash's. The only other dog was a big fuzzy mongrel with a leather collar and bad teeth.

'Mummy,' said a little girl at the end of one of the rows. 'I like that one.' She pointed to a white bull terrier that was sitting sideways, his pink muzzle stuck against the bars. The dog barked frantically.

'Absolutely not!' said her mother, yanking her daughter away. 'That's a pit bull. They're vicious. I wouldn't feel safe with a dog like that in the house. We'll look again next week.'

Mackenzie followed them out of the swing doors. By this time all the dogs were barking. They were barking like maybe they still had a chance. They couldn't read headlines. They didn't know they were public enemy number one.

'Well,' said the girl at the front desk. 'Any luck?'

'No,' said Mackenzie. 'My dog has got a white heart on her left ear. Her name's Cash.'

The girl thought about that. 'Left ear, eh? I'm going to let you check the hospital. We're not supposed to let the public in there, so it'll have to be quick.'

Mackenzie followed her through another door. There were three white cells. The first was empty. In the second there was a small grey dog. She was missing a leg, and her stump had a white bandage. It didn't stop her from wagging her tail, though. The third dog was sleeping. It was a pit bull. It was so thin you could count every rib. Its head looked much too big for the rest of it.

'What's wrong with it?' whispered Mackenzie. The dog had a funnel-like collar strapped around its neck. The face had deep gashes. Most of one ear was ripped away.

'That your dog?' the girl said. 'Some of his ear's missing, so you might not recognize him.'

Mackenzie looked again. 'No,' he said, 'that's not Cash.'

The girl motioned for him to go out. 'Good thing. That one's probably not going to make it. Lost too many fights, I reckon. Someone left him to die behind a pound shop. The shop owner called us.'

'Looks like you're taking good care of him,' said Mackenzie. His knees were shaking.

'We have to hold him nine days. 'Course, as soon as the law's changed, we'll put a dog like that down right away. All the others out the back will be euthanized too. I bet this place will be practically empty for a while.'

She went back behind her desk and picked up some papers. ''Course, the cages will fill up again. People will find another tough-dog breed. Then some child will get bitten and the public will go hysterical all over again. We'll have people lining up to dump the family pet they've raised from a pup. Oh, you can bet those cages won't stay empty for long.'

She shuffled the papers some more. 'Some of the staff have been here a long while. They've seen it happen two or three times. The public picks the new flavour of the month, and some other breed gets the death sentence.'

Most of her rant went over Mackenzie's head. He was thinking of the injured dog. The drugs had let it sleep. It looked as if it would rather just stay that way. As if waking up hurt too much. Maybe it would get its wish.

Maybe Cash was hurting right now. Maybe no one would find her in time. He had to ask. 'What will happen if that pit bull makes it?'

The girl sniffed. 'Who's going to want a beaten-up dog that's been trained to fight? And ninety quid on top. It's a goner one way or the other. Pretty raw deal, eh?' She looked at Mackenzie and bit her lip. 'Sorry, kid. No use fretting over that. You can't change human nature.'

Mackenzie started for the door. 'Check again sometime,' the girl called. 'Here's our card. I'll keep an eye out for your dog.'

Mackenzie phoned her twice a day after that.

Finally she said, 'Look, kid, that dog's gone. You've got to accept it.'

FOURTEEN

Autumn came. Mackenzie went back to school.

Miss Smithers had a word with his new teacher, Mr Hu. 'Mackenzie lives in his own world. Doesn't mix much with the other boys, although they all think he's OK. A call home might keep the dad on his toes, but mind you don't give him any reason to go after the boy. Mackenzie's got enough on his plate.'

During the science lesson Mr Hu demonstrated an experiment for the students. He twirled two eggs. 'Behold!' he exclaimed. 'Now, who can explain why this egg wobbles while the other one spins like a top? First person with a good answer gets a treat. Salt provided.'

Hands went up. Mackenzie looked at one egg. He looked right through it.

Mr Hu sighed. Some kids just didn't appreciate a good education.

Mackenzie was thinking about Cash. Usually his brain kept that sort of thinking parcelled up. But that day the package unravelled somehow.

Cash would be a year and a half by now, he thought. If she was still alive.

The worst thing was not knowing. His dad had been in a temper when he'd left with Cash, and he never thought about what he was doing when he was angry. Maybe he'd just tossed Cash out of the car. That was probably what had happened. So the dog would be alone, outside at night for the first time. She'd nose around for a bit, seeing the world in the dark as a new adventure. Then she'd wait for Mackenzie like she always did. She'd wait and wait. And finally she'd realize that he wasn't coming. That he hadn't kept his promise.

Maybe she'd go looking for him.

Mackenzie tried to stop that train of thought. But

it happened anyway. Now that his thoughts were loose, they just took off and he was carried along for the ride. All of his imaginings were bad ...

Maybe Cash started to look for him. She saw someone in a car, maybe someone who looked like he did. She ran out on the street, her tail up. The driver wouldn't be able to stop in time. And Cash would be under the wheels. She'd hear the squeal of brakes and horns. But by then it would be too late.

Or maybe she'd found someone else. Maybe it was not a nice person. Maybe they forgot to feed her, or she stayed thirsty all day, or maybe they didn't care that she had no blanket ...

'Mackenzie,' said Mr Hu. 'Why don't you try giving this egg a spin? It's not cooperating.'

Mackenzie reached over and twirled one of the eggs. It broke in his hand. The yolk greased his fingers.

'The answer is revealed!' exclaimed Mr Hu. 'That egg is raw. The internal fluid needs time and energy to start spinning. The other egg is hard-boiled. It's solid all the way through, so all of it starts spinning at the same time. Mackenzie, you can eat the cooked one, for your trouble.'

Mr Hu gave him a packet of salt and Mackenzie peeled the shell off the egg and ate it. An idea was growing in his mind. Maybe Cash was alive. Maybe she was managing to survive somehow on the streets. He had to stop moping. He had to find her.

That night he sat on the bottom step of the stairs and waited. When his dad stumbled in just after eight, Mackenzie stood up. 'I want to know what you did with Cash,' he said.

'That dog's long gone,' muttered O'Rourke. 'I'm sick of hearing about it.'

Mackenzie squared up to his dad. 'She was mine. You've got to make up for what you did. Where is she?'

'I don't know where she is.' He pushed past Mackenzie and stomped up the stairs.

'I won't stop asking,' Mackenzie said flatly.

'You're just as daft as your mother if you think I give a damn,' O'Rourke shot back.

'She was my dog. She didn't hurt anyone. Who did you give her to?'

O'Rourke walked across the landing. 'I took her out to the country. She's probably teamed up with the sheep. Been more than half a year. Let it go.'

The bathroom door slammed shut.

Mackenzie stood looking up the stairs. He didn't believe his dad. He must have dumped her in town. And she never got to the shelter. That was either because she was alive or because she wasn't. He'd find out for sure. One way or the other.

Mackenzie went up to his room. He did his maths. He wrote up the physical properties of a raw egg compared to a hard-boiled one. Then he got out his wide marker and some old paper. He began to make posters.

He wrote:

LOST
Pit bull
Female
Brown and white
One ear brown with a white heart

Then he stopped. What now? He didn't have a phone. His father had a mobile, but it was no use anyone calling that. Mackenzie would be the last to know.

Finally Mackenzie put down the number of the

shelter. He'd start checking there again.

He put the posters on the street lamps around his house. But he'd picked a bad time. That night the newspapers carried another story of a pit bull attack. The victim, a little girl, had needed nine stitches. The dog had run away and the police shot it when it was finally cornered in a bus shelter. The eleven o'clock news showed the body being hauled away.

The next morning Mackenzie's posters had all been torn down. All except one. Someone had scribbled the word KILLER in red marker across the page.

FIFTEEN

The nights became a cold injury. One day Cash stopped sleeping on the pile of old mattresses and shoved her body between them instead. Even when temperatures dipped below freezing, she managed to stay warm. Her breath left icy fantasies over the window.

The cold made it harder to find food. Sometimes it was buried in ice. Cash had grown over the summer, and now she had to roam half the night to fill her insides. And she needed even more to keep her warm. She celebrated the first snowfall behind the restaurants where the skips offered the best pickings. By now her teeth and jaws were as strong as iron clamps. She was able to peel the meat off a bone and chew the gristle. And there was always hope of finding rice, or perhaps noodles or potato.

Maybe Cash would have starved. Maybe she would have become too desperate to be careful. Maybe the dog warden would have caught up with her.

Instead she found Abi. Or maybe it was the other way around.

Abi spotted the dog from the train on her way home one Tuesday night. She was staring out of the open window as usual, even though the air was frigid. The cold wind whipped her hair into ghosts.

That first time, she had made no sense of the white spots floating through the weeds. But the next time, Cash ran closer to the track. The lights from the train turned her coat into a patchwork of white and gold.

'It's a dog,' breathed Abi. 'And it's white and tan. It's just like me.'

That was true. Abi was a two-toned young woman. She had skin fair as a winter rose – mostly. But on one cheek she had a patch of brown richer than toffee. That patch spilled down along her neck and her shoulder, sugaring her skin all the way down to the tip of one hand. So there she was, white and brown, like maple syrup drizzled over vanilla ice-cream.

Lots of people stared at Abi because of her colouring. A freak, some said. Drop-dead gorgeous, said others.

The next time she rode past on the train, Abi waited for the dog to come running out of the scrub and snow. It was pony-legged, and thin. There wasn't a collar. It was nobody's dog.

'Dog,' she yelled. 'Good dog!' She tossed her peanut butter sandwich out of the window. The sandwich never hit the ground. The dog jumped up and grabbed for the food as it sailed over the tracks.

Cash hadn't had that kind of food for a long time. She ate every bit, her tongue working hard to unstick her jaws. Lying between her mattresses later on, the memory of it made her whimper in her sleep. Her dreams were drenched in peanut butter and boy.

After that Abi always asked her mother for an extra sandwich. Abi was all skin and bone, so her mum was happy to comply. She didn't know her daughter had fallen for a stray. 'We could pick you up at the hospital and go out to eat afterwards,' she ventured lightly.

Abi laughed. 'All I need is another sandwich, Mum. I like taking the train.'

Cash became a train fan too. Every night the dog would pace alongside the track until the train got to the field. She got to know which nights the girl would be on board, and which nights the window near the back stayed empty. Cash ran alongside every night anyway. There was always hope.

Of course, Mrs Brody saw Cash too. She and Abi had been sharing a wave for more than a year, every Sunday, Tuesday and Thursday. So Mrs Brody saw the dog jumping for the sandwich.

The old lady gave her glasses a good wipe. Her eyes weren't what they used to be, and she wasn't sure that they weren't playing tricks on her. But the dog was still there.

After that, when Mrs Brody waited for Abi, she watched the dog watching for the train. She held her breath every time the dog jumped for the food. And on the days when Abi wasn't aboard, she watched the dog running and hoping.

It gave her an idea.

The next Wednesday Mrs Brody got out her frying pan. The bacon had been in the freezer for a long time, but it looked just fine. Mrs Brody fried up four rashers for herself. That was all she could fit in the pan. Then she cooked four more strips. She made two pieces of toast and poured the bacon fat over them. She made two more just the same. The second lot was for heating up again later.

Dinner was delicious. When the Meals-on-Wheels lady stopped by, Mrs Brody spoke up.

'You don't need to stop by so often, Sarah,' she said. 'I think I'll take up cooking again. Bit of work'll do me good.'

Miss Smithers smiled. 'Just be careful with that old stove, Mrs Brody. This tired house isn't what it used to be.'

Mrs Brody patted her hand. 'You're a comfort to me, dear. I'll be fine.'

Later that night, as Cash ran alongside the empty window of the train, the scent of bacon perfumed the air. She swerved across the field, following her nose. It was a cold night, there was snow everywhere, but it wasn't hard to find the prize. The hot fat steamed on the back step of the first house past the field.

Normally Cash stayed away from houses like that. The light shining from an upstairs window made her hesitate. But the temptation was too great.

The hot bacon and bread slipped down easily. It left her insides all aglow. Afterwards Cash headed for her mattress, catching a mouthful of snow along the way to cool the salt.

In an upstairs window a curtain slipped back into place. Mrs Brody was pleased. She stayed looking at the cold tracks for a long time before she turned out her light.

PC Dean, who was doing his nightly drive down Chester Street, couldn't figure it out. It was the first time he'd seen Mrs Brody stay up late.

Four houses down the street a dog panted on a treadmill. It ran and ran. The other dog watched through the cage. He eyed the water and the food. They were just out of reach.

Then suddenly they were in the cage and he had his fill.

SIXTEEN

'Take the chain off first. No point wasting it.'
Darren's uncle stuffed the broken body of the dog into a rubbish bag and heaved it into the skip. He was in a foul mood. Now he only had one dog left, and it was in bad shape. Probably only good for another fight or two.

Darren stared at the ripped-up carcass of a badger lying in the centre of the warehouse yard. The animal looked pretty big, maybe close to twelve kilos. It had taken the dog some time to finish it off. Then the dog upped and died too. The fight was a draw.

The ring organizer, Sojo, leaned against his silver

BMW counting the night's takings. He was wrapped in a long tweed coat and sporting a cigar. His driver stood next to him, watching the cars leave one by one. Darren thought that maybe the driver carried a firearm, although the stun gun was the only thing out on display.

Darren waited until his uncle steered his pick-up through the gate. Loser, he thought.

'What d'you want, kid?' Sojo muttered. He didn't even look up from his counting.

'What you need,' said Darren, 'is a smart fighting dog.'

Sojo went on counting the notes. He acted as if Darren hadn't spoken.

'Most dogs don't know how to think,' Darren persisted. 'That's why they end up in a skip. You need a dog with brains. Get a dog with brains and give it some teaching, and it'll win every time. You'd get people from all over coming to see it fight.'

Sojo folded up the packet of money. It was a thick wad. 'How big?' he said suddenly.

Darren did some quick guesswork. 'Close to twenty-five kilos,' he said. 'Long legs.'

'Low slung's better,' the man snorted. 'Those

leggy ones tie themselves in knots.'

Darren smirked. 'This one moves like a dancer,' he said. 'You've just got to teach it what's what. The dog's on its own and nobody even knows it's around. I'm telling you, it's smart.'

'You got a dog like that?' The man looked up. 'If you've got a dog like that,' he said, 'you show me. Maybe we can make a deal.'

'You bet, Mr Sojo,' said Darren.

After the BMW left the warehouse yard, Darren headed for the burger place near the empty field. There were fresh tracks in the snow around the bins at the back. Darren eyed them with satisfaction. That dog was going to be his lucky break. All it needed was some time on the treadmill. And a few lessons in manners.

He flicked on his mobile. 'Jake,' he said. 'I've got a business proposition for you. Meet me at my uncle's house tomorrow night. Tell Stuffy to bring some of those potato sacks from his mum's shop.'

Inside the burger bar Darren ordered a double cheese and mushroom melt and pulled out a pencil. Grabbing a napkin he started a list – dog food, can opener, sacks ...

The next night, three dark figures made their way deep into the field from the Chester Street dead end. They found paw prints half a mile in, closer to the river and the old distillery. Jake hauled a cage on a trolley. Stuffy carried the hessian sacking. When they got to an orange tarpaulin flapping in the breeze, they set the cage down and peeled off the covers.

The trap belonged to Darren's uncle. It was nothing more than a stiff wire box with a trigger pad near the rear. When an animal went in for the bait, the door sprang shut.

Darren put on his gloves. He opened a large can of dog food and threw it inside. 'Boys,' he said, 'let's grab some dinner. Chances are there'll be one angry pit bull inside when we get back.'

Cash was waiting for the train. It was Thursday. She loped through the field, cutting past the old tarpaulin. The scent of dog food lured her to the cage. Cash was used to wire of all sorts – wire with barbs, wire in coils, wire mesh and electric cable – so the trap didn't scare her at all. It was just part and parcel of the landscape.

When she went in to lick out the can, the door snapped shut.

Cash didn't make any noise. But she tried hard to get out. By the time Darren and his boys got back, her gums were a bloody mess and the trap was over on its side.

Darren looked at the sight cheerfully. 'Well,' he said. 'Looks like she's learning her first lesson. That bitch can't have her own way no more.' He picked up the sacking and flung it over the mesh.

The journey back was tough. The ground was bumpy and the cage kept falling over. There was no sound from inside.

'There's something wrong with a dog that quiet,' muttered Stuffy. He was breathing hard from trying to keep the cage steady on the trolley as they hauled it between the worst of the ruts and debris. At the edge of Chester Street, they stopped behind a patch of scrub. It was train time. As the train curved with the river and approached the houses, they could see someone at the window, some crazy girl waving at something for all she was worth.

'What's she looking at?' complained Jake.

Darren pointed at the first house. Number one still had lights burning. 'An old woman lives there,' he said. 'Always turns off her lights after the train goes by. We just need to stay here for a minute.'

A long time passed. The lights stayed on. In fact, the whole house lit up.

The boys started grumbling. 'Shut up,' Darren warned, pointing to the street. The boys crouched further behind the scrub as a police car pulled up to the house.

PC Dean got out of his car and rang the doorbell. Then he went inside for a while. When he left, the lights went out. Finally.

'You'd think there was a street party,' Darren complained. 'That old lady picked a bad night to stay up late.'

At least it was dark. They hauled the cage to the back of his uncle's house. Inside the shed they slid up the door of the cage. Cash roared out. She didn't get far. It was just more cage, cramped and cold and empty. The dog in the next cell started barking. When Darren picked up the cattle prod, it stopped and cowered in the corner.

Cash just turned and faced her captors. She growled silently in her head.

Darren leaned close to the bars and grinned. The dog was a prize all right. 'Tomorrow,' he said, 'I'm going to teach you what's what.'

The door of the shed snapped shut. The night grew quiet.

When Abi's father picked her up at the Rooksbury station, Abi was quiet too. 'How are you feeling, love?' he asked as they drove home. He took a quick look at his daughter's face, and his heart ached. She was getting thinner and thinner.

Abi opened her mouth. The dog hadn't shown up and she wanted to tell her dad about it. But she felt that somehow she'd be betraying a secret. She decided to wait.

In the middle of the night Mrs Brody turned on her lights again. She went and checked the back step. The bacon was still there. Wearily she went back to bed.

Mackenzie sat under his covers. He was making new posters. His torch grew dim.

Finally it went out.

SEVENTEEN

The dogfight was scheduled between nightfall and the last train.

The first car to pull into the warehouse yard was a dented old Ford with a souped-up exhaust pipe. A van arrived next, a dirty white one with purple-tinted windows. Darren's uncle followed close behind in the pick-up. Gradually the yard filled up with more vehicles, an old Mercedes, an Austin Mini, some beaten-up Landrovers. The last car to pull around the back was the silver-grey, late-model BMW.

Cash was terrified. She was in a cage in the back of the pick-up under a tarpaulin. The cage jolted back and forth. It offered no place to hide. She jammed her body sideways along one corner for balance. In the dark she smelled fear, not just her own, but the hot distress of the other dog.

Both animals were silent. Both were waiting. One already knew the ropes. But all Cash knew was that she had to get out.

The truck jerked to a stop. Someone pulled back the tarpaulin and heaved the cage onto the pavement. Cash scrambled to right herself in the confined space. As her eyes adjusted to the glare of the lights, she began to pick out faces, a pack of faces, all staring at her.

'She's a good size,' someone said.

'Too pretty to be a fighting dog,' retorted another. 'She doesn't look like she's got experience.'

'Tonight's her first time,' muttered Sojo. He was taking bets now.

Darren spoke up. 'That dog's been on the street for months. A dog like that will take out anything on four legs once she's had a bit of practice. Tonight's her coming-out party.'

Darren's uncle stopped him. 'Don't take any notice of that boy,' he sneered. 'My nephew's a fool.

He can't wait to get the bitch in the ring. That little lady will get a thrashing before she even knows what day it is. I'll give you three-to-one odds my dog will take her out.'

The crowd watched as Darren's uncle hauled the other cage from the back of his truck and opened the door. He yanked on the chain and the dog came out. It was small and ugly, with an oversized jaw and rheumy eyes. One flank had less flesh than the other. It stank.

Someone in the crowd snorted. 'That dog's fighting days are over. Look at him. He walks on that chain like a pup. You his mummy or something?'

Darren's uncle ignored the insult. 'He's learned to behave. And he's got experience. He's a four-times winner. Not like the competition. *She's* greener than new grass. Let's get on with it. Who's betting with me?'

There was a lot of money changing hands for a few minutes. Sojo put it all in a safe in the BMW. Then the men pulled their cars into a circle around the two dogs and their keepers. It was a wild sight, the small circle of vehicles pulled close like wagons round a camp fire, their engines running, clouds of exhaust fumes rising into the dark winter air. The centre was a blaze of headlights. Men and boys leaned against their cars and stared at the two dogs, one still in a cage and the other standing rigid at the end of a cold chain.

Cash looked back through the mesh of her prison, taking stock of the scene in front of her. The lights of the cars and the rising exhaust fumes blinded her. The sounds of the engines muffled the river noises. But she could smell the field, the plastic and the cement.

She'd been there before, checking out the skips. She knew where she was. She stood there, remembering that the back of the yard came up to the fence. She had a chance.

Darren was right about one thing. Cash was a thinking dog.

The wire door of her prison swung open. Cash stayed where she was.

'Get out,' Darren ordered. He was feeling a bit nervous. Maybe he should have waited. Maybe he shouldn't have challenged his uncle. Maybe his uncle was right and the dog needed some prepping. Maybe he should have warmed up the dog's appetite and thrown a squirrel or two in the cage to get her going.

He lost his patience and poked her with the cattle prod. Cash felt a sharp sting at the base of her tail. The second time it happened, she moved out of the cage and into the light of the ring. The men were silent now, slouched against their vehicles getting an eyeful.

Cash looked back warily, her head down. The hot lights trapped the cigarette smoke and the exhaust fumes and the smell of beer.

The electric prod jolted her again, this time so hard she jumped. She took a step forwards, unsure what was expected. She made no sound, not even a silent growl.

There was a sharp bark. The other dog came into her sight.

Sojo signalled to his driver to ready the stun gun. Then he gestured at Darren and his uncle. 'OK, you two. Wake those dogs up.'

Darren prodded Cash again. 'Get out there, you dumb animal. Before that other dog takes off one of your pretty ears.'

The next jolt singed her flank. The men started to jeer.

'Wimps!' someone yelled. 'Wake up. Do your stuff. This isn't a dog show.'

'Kill! Kill! Kill!' another chanted.

The other terrier barked again. He pulled against the lead, turning sideways a little to get a look at his opponent, his right eye still swollen from his last fight. Saliva dripped from his jaw. He already knew that his weekend companion in the shed was the opposition. He already knew he had to fight.

All the while Cash was thinking too. Soon the train would come. She began to pull against her heavy chain, away from the other dog.

The men guffawed. They hooted. 'We came here to see a good fight,' they griped. 'These dogs are having a cosy chat. Where's the action?'

A small boy jumped up and down. 'Get him!' he yelled at Cash. 'Get that ugly useless dog. Rip him to bits!'

The other dog was confused. Cash was sending all the wrong signals. He snarled some more. He barked, fiercely.

Bravely.

Cash hunched. She was ready for anything. But she didn't make a sound. She wasn't looking at the other dog. She was looking across the yard to the back fence.

Darren checked the warehouse front gate. He was in trouble and he knew it. The new dog wasn't going to fight. She was a coward, a sissy. His uncle was right. And that was going to make Sojo really angry. Slowly he backed out of the lights.

Sojo stepped into the circle in front of the men. He was getting aggravated. A red flush crept up his neck over his white scarf. 'They just need a warm-up,' he said. 'Something to get them going.' He gave a signal, and his driver reached into the boot of the car. He pulled out a cat, an old tom. Its front legs were tied together.

'Unhook those brutes,' Sojo commanded.

Darren and his uncle let their dogs loose just as the driver tossed the cat into the air between them.

Both dogs lunged. But Cash was so light on her feet she could have played basketball. She caught the cat in midair and headed straight for the lights of a blue saloon car, her catch swinging from her jaws.

That got everybody excited. The dog looked a whole lot more scary when she was moving. Men scrambled into their cars and trucks. One leaped through an open window and got stuck halfway in with his backside in the air. The driver of the saloon grabbed his screaming son and clambered onto the bonnet of his car.

The BMW driver aimed his stun gun and fired at the running dog, but Cash jumped up and out of range. Instead, the dart hit the dad. He dropped like a stone on top of his boy and they collapsed in a heap across the windscreen. Cash kept on going, right over them. She cleared the boot of the car and raced across the yard.

Darren's uncle snapped a chain on the other dog before it could follow. He kicked at it viciously.

'Get that stun gun ready,' the big man yelled at his driver. 'That dog's not going anywhere. There's three metres high of chain link out there. You shoot her as she circles back. And if you miss this time, you're fired!'

He whirled round. 'And someone close the blasted gate!'

There was no one to do that. The cars were already pulling out. Nobody wanted to be around with a pit bull on the loose. Not a pit bull like that, at any rate.

Cash swerved slightly. She headed straight for the fence – and the hole that she knew was there.

A warehouse worker, looking for a short cut home along the railway track one day, had taken some cutters to the links. And Cash, on a summer's roaming, had discovered the gap. Now she crouched low and rammed herself between the jagged ends. The snow was piled up, so it was a tight fit. One of the tips sliced a thin red line along her flank.

But she was free. She didn't even notice her jaws were still full of cat.

The air was blue with swearing as the cars piled out of the warehouse yard, most of it from Sojo. The night had cost him dearly. Darren had disappeared.

Sojo snarled at Darren's uncle as he climbed into his fancy car. 'Listen, McNab, you'd better make sure I never set eyes on that dog again,' he threatened, gesturing to the dog chained to the truck. 'Or that nephew of yours either.'

Darren's uncle was left alone in the middle of the lot with the dog. He stared at it angrily. Sojo was right. The thing was past redemption. It didn't want to fight any more, that was for sure. He dragged the animal over to the back fence out of sight behind some scrub and chained it to the links. It would be dead soon. It'd make some fox a good dinner.

McNab got into his truck and did some thinking. The night was a dead loss. It was time to move on. He had a friend in Frimpton-by-the-Sea who was looking to set up a ring. The more he thought about it, the better it sounded. His rent was three months overdue anyway. And Darren could go to hell. His brother's kid had sponged off him long enough. Let his parents do the baby-sitting for a change.

McNab drove around the building and through the gate. When he was back on the street, he switched on his lights. He was already planning his exit.

In the dark, the dog sank into the frozen weeds. He shivered.

EIGHTEEN

PC Dean was driving down the old factory road when a pick-up truck with its lights off pulled out of a warehouse yard. That's the guy from number 9 Chester Street, he thought. He pulled his car to the kerb and let the engine idle. The warehouse looked as if it was shut up for the night: the gate was closed and there was a bright security light on over it. Why would anyone be back there after hours? He pulled the car up to the gate and tested the lock. It swung open easily. Out back the yard was empty. Everything looked OK.

PC Dean sighed. It looked OK, but it didn't feel

right. He pulled his torch from the glove compart-
ment and radioed the station. It wouldn't hurt to
have a quick look around. He got out of the car.

Cash got back to her mattresses just as the train
was leaving the station. She dropped her furry
bundle and sprinted back down the stairs. It was
almost train time.

The old tom went limp on the cold covers. He was
shell-shocked. After a long time he sat up and took a
good look at the room. Then he set to work chewing
at the strings that bit into his front paws.

Abi stared anxiously out of the window, scanning
the dark field. If she didn't see the dog this time,
she'd have to tell her dad. She'd make him go back
and help her look. She couldn't wait any longer.

She was running out of time in more ways than
one.

Then she saw the dog running towards the train,
catching up to it and veering to run alongside. 'Oh!'
she cried. 'You're back. You're back.' She tossed her
sandwich out of the narrow slit. 'Good dog,' she
called. 'I love you, dog!'

Cash caught the treat as elegantly as ever. She was
starving. The sandwich was history before the train

and the girl were out of sight. Hopefully, she turned and made for the doorstep of the first house next to the field. All the house lights were on, and someone was standing at the back door. Cash didn't care. She knew it was a safe place.

There was a ham bone waiting. It was still warm.

Mrs Brody stood at the back door and clapped her hands.

By the time Cash got back to her mattresses, the old tom was washing his coat. He had already found a puddle of melted snow dripping in through a broken window and helped himself to a long drink. Now he was waiting for dinner. Cash dropped the ham bone on the floor. The old tom stalked over to it as if he was the King of Siam, and scooped out the marrow with one sore paw. The fat landed in a soft puddle-lump on the floor.

Both animals got busy with dinner. Afterwards they settled inside the mattresses where it was warm and safe.

PC Dean was about to call it a night. He had done a close search of the warehouse grounds, moving his torch carefully back and forth over the pavement. All he had found was a piece of chain – and some beer bottles. Right up by the back fence something shifted in the scrub. Cautiously he moved towards the dark patch between the bushes. A low growl rose up.

PC Dean jumped. His torch picked out the dog chained to the fence, manacled so tightly it couldn't even lie straight. One eye was swollen shut. It smelled foul.

'Dog fighting,' Dean said out loud. He reached for his phone again. 'Cancel the backup. I need a dog warden,' he said. 'Tell them to bring some sedation. I've got a really sick dog here.'

It took about thirty minutes. PC Dean didn't go near the dog. He got his blanket from the car and threw it over the shivering thing. The animal relaxed a bit, and the chain let out some slack.

The warden injected a sedative into the animal right away. As soon as the animal sagged into sleep, he cut the chain. 'It's badly hurt,' he muttered. 'I'd like to get my hands on whoever did this.'

'Now what?' asked PC Dean. He ran his hand over the animal's flank. It was still shivering.

'I'll take it to the shelter,' said the warden. 'They'll put it down as soon as you give us the OK.'

PC Dean got back in his car. He drove down

Chester Street. The house where Darren was staying was dark. The front door was wide open. Dean went through the whole house, top to bottom. There was nothing in there that anybody would want – just a few sticks of furniture and some kitchen scraps. Out in the shed he found an old treadmill, a length of chain, and an empty bucket.

When his shift was over, he drove down to the RSPCA shelter and had a chat with the front desk.

NINETEEN

Cash woke up. She shoved her broad head out from between the lumpy mattresses, and cocked her white ear. It angled back and forth like a satellite dish searching for signals. Her black nose twitched. Satisfied at last, she wriggled out of her covers, leaving an opening that steamed in the cold air. She stood up and planted her front feet wide under her stocky breast. Her tail swung back and forth slowly, the white tip curving over her narrow withers. Dusty sun splashed over her coat. She was shiny, she was all shine, her coat as sleek as satin, her eyes black marbles.

Half brindle, half white, a patch over one eye, she was all dog. She was twenty-six kilos of shiny pit bull.

Both ears went up.

The tom cat entered the room, dragging a dead rat. It was almost as big as he was. The cat dropped the rat on the floor right in front of Cash.

Cash eyed the carcass. She wasn't hungry. She turned to look out of the window. As she watched, grey clouds moved in and the sun drained away from the room. The long cut on her rump began to bleed, the fresh red seeping along the crusty wound.

The cat licked it clean. Then he eased into the cave of old mattress. Inside it was still warm. He curled up and closed his eyes. The mattress purred.

After a while Cash went back to bed too.

On Tuesday night Mrs Brody and Abi Waters got the shock of their lives. The dog showed up to run with the train as usual, but she had company. Two animals flew along the tracks. Abi fumbled with the sandwich, and it hit the lip of the window and fell back to the floor. She swiped up the pieces and threw the lot again. The bits went flying. In amazement she watched the animals jump for the food, a *pas de deux* of cream and gold, and night smoke.

Mrs Brody stood on her cold back doorstep and clapped her hands again.

TWENTY

When Mrs Brody went to bed, she dreamed about the animals.

Down in the kitchen her kettle cooled. Behind the walls an old wire cooled too.

The wire was worn out. Each day it heated and cooled, heated and cooled. Sometimes it got so hot it glowed. The heat of it charred the insides of the old wall plaster and toasted it brown. The sharp smell of smoke inside the walls never found a way out.

Each day the glow stretched towards the heavy cobwebs strung between the joists. They were fuel to the glow.

Mrs Brody dreamed all night long.

Saturday came, and so did Meals-on-Wheels. Miss Smithers bought Mrs Brody dinner – a beef stew with parsnips and turnips, a soft white bun, and apple crumble. When she carried the tray into Mrs Brody's house, she caught a sharp scent, like a match just struck. It was gone before she had time to think. While the stew was warming on the stove, she checked the living room. It smelled fresh. It looked good too, the knick-knacks dusted and the pillows plumped. Back on the stove, the stew came to a bubble.

Mrs Brody pronounced the dinner delicious.

She's looking better, thought Miss Smithers. The house was too. There were groceries in the cupboard and a bowl of tulip bulbs on the sideboard, their tips peeping out of the soil. Miss Smithers gave the old woman a hug when she said goodnight. 'Shall I put the kettle on before I go?' she asked.

'Now, now,' said Mrs Brody. 'Don't go spoiling me, Sarah. I'll get a cup later.'

They waved goodbye and Mrs Brody went back to her living room to watch TV. Half an hour before train time, she went to the kitchen and put the left-over stew on the work surface by the door. She plugged in the kettle too. After the water came to the boil, she pulled the plug and poured the water over a tea bag. Then she hurried back to the living room. The news was on.

The kettle woke up the wire, and a red heat travelled along the strand. It shot right into the spiders' hard work. The slender web necklaces turned into tiny filaments of white-hot ash. They broke and scattered. Nearby a label pasted to an old beam flamed up. Red tongues licked the splinters in the wood hungrily. Soon full flames embraced the beam itself. The fire was getting an appetite.

Mrs Brody couldn't take her eyes off the news. There had been another pit bull attack. A neighbour said the owner used to leave the two dogs in the back garden for days. They were cold and hungry when the three-year-old had wandered out of her front garden after a ball. The child had had to have twenty-seven stitches in his arm. Doctors thought he might lose one of his fingers.

The dogs had been removed and the owner charged with criminal negligence. On camera he complained that it was the victim who was to blame for the attack: the child had unlatched his gate. 'The dogs were just protecting my property,' he declared. 'People shouldn't have kids if they can't look after them.'

An outraged politician said that the pit bull ban should be rushed through council without delay.

When a picture of the two animals flashed up on the screen, Mrs Brody got quite a shock. One of them looked just like the dog that ran with the train. Well I never, she thought. Dogs are like people. All the same, and as different as day and night.

The weather report came on. Weather didn't matter much when you never went out, and Mrs Brody dozed during the forecast. Afterwards she made for the kitchen. It was nearing train time. Time to put the stew out for the animals. Both of them.

She walked through the swing doors of the kitchen, right into a wall of smoke. Mrs Brody's old lungs shut down instantly. There wasn't time to get out. She slumped to the floor.

Across the back field Abi held on to the back of her seat, gripping her sandwich, watching the scenery flash by. There they were! Her dog was running across the field, the white patches of its coat steaming through the scrub. The cat was dashing back and forth at its heels.

Cash yelped joyously when she spotted Abi. She veered to run with the train.

'Good dog!' yelled Abi. She flung the food.

Cash jumped for the sandwich. But she got a whiff of smoke just as her feet left the ground. She twisted round in midair. The sandwich fell into a leftover patch of snow.

Cash was already headed for the first house on the street.

Abi saw the smoke snaking out through the back door of Mrs Brody's home at the same time. Frantically she grabbed for her mobile and dialled 999. 'There's a fire,' she said. 'I'm on the train just past the housing estate west of the station. The house backs on to the tracks. There's smoke coming out of the back door. An old lady lives there all by herself. Hurry!'

At the word 'fire', the operator relayed the call to the police and the fire station. They jumped into action. It took the firefighters twenty-seven seconds to pull out of the station. An ambulance was on the road half a minute later.

PC Dean made it to the house first. The smoke was already slipping out of the windows and doors. Grabbing his crowbar, he ran up the front steps and attacked the lock. Then he put his boot to the door. When it gave way, great choking masses of electrical smoke poured out. PC Dean could feel his throat closing. He fell to his knees and pulled at the buttons of his uniform.

He needed to cover his face and get into that house!

Something inside shoved him hard and he fell heavily against the door frame. An animal was hauling someone through the front door. It was Mrs Brody. Blindly PC Dean moved forward, groping for an arm or a leg so he could help, and together they dragged the old woman down the steps and into the fresh night air.

PC Dean collapsed just as the fire engine screamed up to the house. An ambulance pulled up alongside. Two paramedics jumped out and clapped an oxygen mask on the old woman. Then they fixed one on PC Dean. The firefighters entered the house, loaded down with pickaxes and extinguishers. The hungry fire behind the back wall was snuffed out well before it got on to its main course.

One of the firefighters brought a cat out. It was hanging limply from his arm. 'We'll drop this old tom at the vet's,' he said. 'If that lady makes it, she'll be wanting her pet.'

At the hospital PC Dean woke up on a trolley in the corridor of the A & E department with a doctor standing over him. 'You're OK to go home in a couple of hours,' the doctor said. 'Your throat may be a bit raspy for a few days, but it'll clear.'

'What about Mrs Brody?' PC Dean croaked.

The doctor smiled. 'It looks like she'll make it. Another minute in that smoke and it would have been a different story. You're a hero.'

'Not me,' said PC Dean. 'It was a pit bull.'

TWENTY-ONE

Jimmy Cormorant was a new reporter with a first-time job doing local stories for *City News*. Fires were old news. But the pit bull angle was too good to pass up.

Jimmy followed up the story. He and a cameraman went to Chester Street and filmed Mrs Brody's house. They interviewed everyone they could get their hands on. When his news editor previewed the story, he was so pleased he gave Jimmy some air time on the evening news.

The story was a lucky break for that young news hound. Pit bulls were on everybody's mind. And the story of a pit bull *hero* gave a whole new twist to the subject. Jimmy was finally where he'd always wanted to be: in front of the camera with a big story that would tug at the heart strings of every man, woman and child.

The news report played over and over, all night long. WONDER DOG COMES TO THE RESCUE! It wasn't long before the whole city was paying attention. A mystery pit bull had pulled an old woman from her burning house.

The TV camera panned the neighbourhood as Jimmy interviewed some of the neighbours. No one in Chester Street knew who owned the dog, although some people said they had heard the odd bark late at night.

The policeman who had been first on the scene, a PC Dean, declined to speculate on the whereabouts of the mystery dog, other than to say the animal was dragging the woman out of the house when he arrived on the scene. He had helped the dog to take Mrs Brody down the front steps. Dean added, 'Someone on the train saw the smoke and phoned 999. I hope she'll come forward. The police would like to commend her personally.'

Firefighters confirmed that they had had a brief glimpse of the dog skirting around the back of the house as they had pulled up. 'It was a pit bull all right,' one of them said. 'Light and fast. Didn't give us any time to say thanks.'

Jimmy interviewed the doctor as well. 'The patient was in acute respiratory distress. A few more seconds in that smoke would have caused irreparable damage to her lungs,' the doctor stated. 'The quick action of that dog saved her life.'

As the city watched, Jimmy stood in Mrs Brody's front garden and summed up the story. Behind him the empty field stretched into the night. The distillery was just a black blot on the horizon.

'Tonight a mysterious animal appeared out of nowhere and put itself at risk to save a human life,' Jimmy went on. 'The irony is that the animal is a pit bull, a species the public loves to hate. Soon this breed will be banned from the city. Let us hope that the Wonder Dog finds a safe refuge before that fatal hour arrives … This is Jimmy Cormorant, reporting for *City News*, live from Chester Street.'

Mackenzie stood in the front room watching the TV report. His dad was sprawled across the couch.

'It's Cash,' Mackenzie said. His voice was hard and flat. 'I know it's Cash. That's where you dumped her, isn't it? In that old field between here and the train station.'

His father switched to a sitcom and took a swig of beer. Maybe he should have another look for that dog, he thought. It might finally be worth some *real* cash. 'Better mind your mouth,' he said out loud.

Miss Smithers was also watching the news. She put down her tea and let her mind go back to Mackenzie and his dad. She was still thinking when the story of the pit bull came up on another channel twenty minutes later. Miss Smithers knew Jimmy Cormorant. She had gone to school with him. She'd ring him tomorrow. First, though, she'd go and see Mrs Brody at the hospital. Maybe she'd even take a walk down Chester Street. PC Dean just might pass by.

Ratings for *City News* skyrocketed. 'Jimmy,' his editor said the next day, 'that story is a big hit with the public. The way I see it, you've got to find that dog. Keep the story alive in the meantime.'

Jimmy was only too happy to follow orders. He went to his computer and did a search. He was astonished at the number of hits for famous pit bulls.

Weela, Stubby, Norton, and Cheyenne … Even Helen Keller had a pit bull. Nubs, Porky, Mr Barton, and Smokes … And the military used the breed! He would do a series on pit bull heroes. Track down some of their owners if he could. It was time to make those old stories fresh news.

He'd talk to some victims of pit bull attacks too. A good reporter gave both sides of the story. All that would be enough to keep things stirred up while he nosed around Chester Street. His editor was right. He had to find that dog.

Mackenzie skipped school the next day. It was time he did more than make posters.

As he walked all the way down Chester Street towards the vacant field, he felt a new hope. He would cover every inch of the street, and every frozen foot of the field. He'd search the winter out if he had to. He'd find his dog, or end up in the river trying.

TWENTY-TWO

Abi Waters' mum was making sandwiches. Her daughter was about to head into the city for her last dialysis session. The hospital had found a donor kidney.

It was now or never.

The doctor had been clear with the Waters family. 'We've found a match,' he explained carefully. 'The kidney belongs to a middle-aged woman who suffered massive head injuries in an accident. She's on the organ donation list, and her next of kin have agreed to let us proceed. It's Abi's best chance for a normal life.' The doctor had looked at her carefully then. 'It's your decision, Abi. There are always risks with a transplant. Your body might reject the donor organ despite our best efforts. And there's always a chance of infection with any surgery.'

Abi hadn't even hesitated. 'It's my life,' she declared firmly. 'I'll take the chance.'

'Your dad and I are going to drive you to the hospital tonight, Abi,' her mother said, packing a drink in with the food. 'We'll feel better doing that.'

Abi tried to focus on her mother's words. But she was watching the news on the TV screen in the living room. Jimmy Cormorant was talking about the 'Wonder Dog'. 'That's great, Mum,' she said. 'But ... we'll have to make a stop on the way home. I'd better go and find Dad. There's something I need to tell you both.'

When her mum and dad were seated at the table, Abi began, 'You see, there's this dog ...'

Kid O'Rourke slipped an envelope into a post box. It was addressed to Mackenzie.

Mack,
It's me, Kid. I'm not too far away. I've got a job in the city at a hospital. I'm back in college part time

too. Sorry about ditching you like that. I've met someone at the clinic, and she's been telling me what I've known all along. We've got to stick together. You and me. I've got myself a rented room with a cooker and I think maybe you ought to come and stay with me. Hope you're OK. I expect that with me gone, the old man's tormenting you.

Think about it. I'll come round soon. Kid

The letter arrived on Monday. O'Rourke saw it first. He tore open the envelope and read it. Afterwards he screwed up the paper in his fist. Who did that loser think he was? The letter went in the bin.

A few hours later O'Rourke had second thoughts. The letter just might be his big break. He fished it out of the bin and spread it open on the table, right where Mackenzie would see it. Then he grabbed his car keys.

Jane would be home soon. He'd pick up some Scotch. A few roses wouldn't hurt either.

He knew how to be a gentleman.

TWENTY-THREE

The kids of Mortimer Street were going to have a big night out. They were going to drink. They had stuffed a shopping bag full of half-empty bottles pinched from the cupboards and cabinets of their families.

One of the kids was just old enough to have a driving licence. 'I'm going to a film,' he said to his mum. 'Can I have the car?'

His mother had a migraine. It had been a tough week. A few hours in a quiet house sounded good to her. 'Mind you be home by eleven,' she grunted.

'Absolutely,' he said. 'No problem, Mum.'

He picked the other guys up at the café. One of them pulled out an extra bottle from his jacket. 'It's vodka. Seriously strong stuff,' he announced. 'And still half left. My dad's had it in the cellar for years. He'll never miss it.'

The kids took the car up a side street all the way to where it ended, at the barrier that stretched in front of the tracks and the river. The house to one side had a tall wooden fence running around the back garden, and the driver squeezed the car off the road and around the barrier, finally managing to wedge the car between the fence and the tracks. He stopped in a patch of weed. It was already dark and the car's lights lit up the track and the fence and the scrub along the river bank.

'No one will see us here,' he laughed.

'We're half on the rails,' one of the other boys complained. 'What if there's a train?'

'I've been living by these rails my whole life,' the driver scoffed. 'Only one train left tonight. Comes after eleven. We'll be long gone by then. I've got to get the car back or my mum will kill me.' He fished under the seat for the bag and took out a whisky bottle.

'It's time to party!'

One swallow set him choking.

The others laughed. They passed the bottles around, draining each one dry. Pretty soon they were sprawled all over the seats. They fell asleep. The car headlights shone steadily.

Twenty minutes later the battery died.

Cash was on her nightly prowl. The car on the tracks was a puzzle. She pranced back and forth, and finally put her front paws up against the window to get a better look. The thump on the door shook the driver half awake.

'Holy sh …,' he stuttered when he opened his eyes. 'Wake up, you guys. Look at that thing.' He turned the key. But the ignition just clicked.

The other boys stirred. 'Whaz that?' one of them muttered. His head throbbed. All he could see was steam on the window. He took a swipe and peered out.

Cash took off as soon as the boys woke up. She loped a hundred metres down the track and dipped over the river bank. She waited for the car to move off. When it stayed put, she ran back and jumped on to the bonnet.

All the boys were wide awake then. They started to bang on the windows. The driver tried the ignition again. But the car just sat there silent.

Cash slipped down the bank and waited a little longer.

The boys waited too. They were feeling pretty rough. They needed the toilet. One of them threw up. The smell of vomit filled the car. It was the last straw. Three of them piled out of the car and ran off, yelling insults at each other. The last one slumped against the back seat and closed his eyes. He was too dizzy to even fall out of the door.

Cash paid no attention to the boys. She looked at the car. She turned the other way and stared down the railway tracks. Her ears tilted this way and that. The night was quiet. The seconds ticked away. It was almost train time.

She started to run.

The train sat in the station, filling up with night travellers. Darren got into the first carriage and sagged into a window seat. He looked at the other passengers. There was nobody there he knew. It was the only good luck in a bad couple of days. His uncle had moved out. That would have been fine if the landlord hadn't come banging on the door, demanding his rent arrears. The heating was switched off soon after.

Darren shrugged and slouched further into his seat. He'd have to go home for a bit, that was all. His parents were wimps. They would take him in. He'd stay for a few weeks, get some new clothes and work out his next move.

Downtown, Abi climbed into the back of her parents' car. The night nurses had had a little party for her at the end of the dialysis session. The young man from security had come by too, and he and Abi had shared a quick kiss under her parents' eyes. Abi left the hospital full of warm wishes.

In two days she would be in the operating theatre.

Her dad started the car. Abi and her mother sat silently in the back seat as he pulled out of the car park. They headed for Chester Street.

TWENTY-FOUR

Cash was aiming to stop a train.

She hurled herself down the tracks like a river in spring flood. It took her six minutes to get to the station. When she got there, she stopped on the tracks just out of range of the lights. Her sides heaved as she struggled to catch her breath. There was more to do.

The driver looked at the tracks ahead. All clear. He blasted the whistle and eased his engine away from the glare of the platform. As the train's headlight flooded the tracks ahead, he saw the dog. It was jumping up and down, doing a solo dance on the rails, trying to

138

grab a strip of air with its paws. As the driver stared, it whirled around and began to run down the track.

'There's a dog on the tracks,' he said.

The driver's mate saw the dog too. He laughed. 'That thing will get out of the way when we're on its tail. Let's get going.'

The driver let the train out a little. But the dog stayed on the tracks. Soon it was running flat out.

The train picked up speed. In ten seconds it would be on the animal.

The dog struggled to stay in front. The gap closed.

That's when the driver pulled on the brake.

The train slowed dramatically. All along the cars, people felt the tug. They stared out of the windows anxiously. Newspapers fluttered to the floor. In the first carriage Darren felt sweat trickle down the back of his neck.

'What the hell are you doing?' said the driver's mate. 'It's just a dog. A stupid one. We've got a schedule to keep to.'

'That's a pit bull,' declared the driver, still holding the train in check. 'Don't you watch the news? Maybe it's the Wonder Dog. I've got a gut feeling something's up.'

Both men saw the car on the tracks at the same time. Both men hit the emergency brakes. The train screeched. Sparks flew off the rails as twenty tons of iron grabbed hold. The front end stopped ten feet short of the car. And just shy of the dog.

'Whew,' said the mate. 'That was a close shave.'

'A miracle, more like,' said the driver. 'We'd have been thrown off the track for sure.'

The boy in the back seat of the car never even woke up.

Most of the passengers stayed in their seats, their noses pressed to the glass. One woman started to cry. A few people got up and stuck their heads out of the doors between the carriages. They didn't see Darren slip out and run down the river bank.

Darren wasn't taking any chances. Maybe the police were after him. There was no other reason for the train to stop in the middle of nowhere.

Cash headed for the cover of the river scrub too. She collapsed, grabbing for air. A few moments later, the dog heaved herself up and followed the river away from the train. She saw Darren but she didn't care. She just trotted past him. That scared Darren so much, he jumped in the freezing cold water.

The driver stood between the back garden fences and his train. He stared at the car parked on the tracks. The dog had disappeared. 'If someone tried to tell me that a dog could stop my train,' he muttered, 'I'd have called him a fool. I suppose seeing is believing.'

Cash was running again. She made her way back to Mrs Brody's house cautiously, hoping for some food. There was still a strong smell of burnt wood in the air. That and something else. Peanut butter.

'Dog,' a voice whispered. A girl stood at the edge of the field. 'Dog,' the girl whispered again.

Cash backed up a little and braced herself. Her tail waved slowly. Her body shook. Her eyes went past the girl to the two people behind her.

Mr and Mrs Waters hung back. But Mr Waters had a cricket bat. Just in case. He wasn't going to let anything hurt his daughter.

'Dog.' The girl stepped a little closer. She waited respectfully.

Cash fretted. She sat down. She tilted her head. Finally her paw came up. She started to wave it in the air.

Abi got down on her knees. She stretched out her

hand until there was just half a metre of space between them.

Cash crept a little closer. She stuck out her nose.

Abi leaned in. The dog's nose was cold and dry.

That little tickle broke the ice. Cash flopped on her back and stuck up her belly. She was such a good dog.

Abi gave Cash a tummy rub. She scratched Cash's snout. She whispered in her ear. Then she got the sandwich out of her bag. 'I've got to go, dog,' Abi said. 'I'll be gone for a while. Wait for me.'

Her mother pressed her lips together. Finally she turned to Abi's dad. 'Maybe we could take the dog home,' she whispered.

'No,' Mr Waters said. He dropped the cricket bat to wipe a tear from his eye. 'That dog's an angel. You can't take an angel home.'

TWENTY-FIVE

Jimmy worked on the story all night long. The news of the narrowly averted train crash broke at six o'clock the next morning. Once again his was the first item on the news. He stood in front of the train, the camera angled so that viewers could see just how close it had come to the parked car.

The train driver had lots to say for the cameras. 'It's the first time in four years that I haven't kept my train on schedule. The dog refused to give up. I think I'd have run it over before it'd have left the tracks. That dog's a hero.'

The driver's mate agreed. 'We knew straight away

that that dog was trying to tell us something.'

Even the daily papers had the story splashed over the first page:

WONDER DOG AVERTS TRAIN TRAGEDY

People shook their heads. It was incredible. The Wonder Dog had performed another miracle. It had faced down a train.

Jimmy kept pumping up the story as the day wore on. He fleshed out the details. The four boys who had been in the car were rounded up and questioned by the police. Their names were withheld due to their ages. A parent claimed the boys had stopped the car because of engine trouble. He said that the pit bull had made the kids run away.

One of the kids soon put the story straight. 'I don't remember much,' he mumbled. 'We were drunk. I threw up. It was gross. The car wouldn't start, so we ditched it.'

The empty bottles and the vomit found in the car supported his words. So did the boy in the back seat. Once he sobered up.

As Jimmy signed off, he left his viewers with something to think about.

'Bylaw 132 was written to remove a dangerous

breed from our streets. In three days' time Bylaw 132 will become law throughout the region. In three days, at midnight, countless pit bulls in animal shelters across the city will receive a death sentence. Puppies born after tomorrow will be destroyed. But the public is now left to wonder about this law after the strange events of the last week. A mystery pit bull has become a public hero. Is this dog trying to send us a message?'

Then Jimmy strayed from his script. He gestured helplessly to the camera. 'The shelters are full of pit bulls. Anybody out there want a dog before it's too late?'

The editor almost sacked Jimmy on the spot. Good reporters, he grumbled, keep their personal opinions out of it. The only thing that saved Jimmy's job was the public reaction to his plea. That day people went to the animal shelters across the city in record numbers. They all wanted to adopt a pit bull or a lookalike.

The shelters rose to the challenge. They vetted each application carefully. Most of the prospective owners were good fits: single people with a liking for animals and a sense of responsibility. More than half the requests were approved.

Nine of the people who wanted to take a dog had been on the train Cash had stopped the previous night.

The driver of the train stopped by the RSPCA. 'I'm afraid of dogs,' he said to the girl at the desk. 'I've got a friend who almost lost his leg to a rottweiler. So I can't quite work out how I feel about last night.'

He gave the society a hundred-pound donation. He didn't know how he felt. But the donation made him feel better.

TWENTY-SIX

Darren spent a long night in a coffee shop nursing his wet feet. Every time the staff looked as though they were about to kick him out, he bought another doughnut. The headline in the morning paper perked him up. Maybe he wouldn't have to go home after all.

If I find that dog, he thought, I'll be a hero. It might be worth some cash too. The hard part would be catching her. The dog was too smart to fall for the cage trick twice. Darren checked out his rucksack. His uncle's stun gun was there, along with a length of chain. It was enough.

Stuffy and Jake would be in school by now. He'd wander over and grab them later.

He walked over to Chester Street. It looked like a circus had come to town, full of reporters and cameramen and gawkers. The house he lived in with his uncle already had a padlock on the door. Darren walked straight past. He didn't want anybody asking him questions. And he certainly didn't want his picture on the news. No way.

He spent the rest of the afternoon exploring the field. It was pretty bleak. There didn't seem to be anywhere for a big dog to take cover. All the warehouses had something going on during the day. The only place to hide out was the old distillery.

The more Darren thought about it, the more sense that made. He'd take the guys along after dark. If the dog was there, they'd flush her out. He'd spend the rest of the day working out how to get inside.

At eight o'clock, all three of them went to the field. Jake and Stuffy were uneasy. They weren't sure that tangling head-on with a Wonder Dog was a good idea. The empty building highlighted by the moon was enough to give anyone the heebie-jeebies. Even Darren shivered when he crossed the tracks. He took a quick look along the rails to make sure there was no pit bull bearing down on him.

'Follow me,' he whispered, veering around the high brick sides to the back of the distillery. The night light reflected in the thick oily surface of the river. Broken bits of glass glittered amongst the weeds.

'Blimey, Darren,' complained Stuffy. 'You sure that dog's here?'

''Course I'm sure,' Darren bragged. 'And I found a way inside while you blokes were sleeping through history. Come on.'

One at a time they crawled through the gap where a plank was missing from the swing door, and headed up the ramp. Darren aimed his torch into the tunnel ahead. The ramp opened onto a steel walkway suspended over the distillery cellar. They stepped onto it gingerly, their footsteps sending up hollow echoes in the damp air. After a couple of metres they stopped and looked over the edge, trying to see into the murk. There was water dripping somewhere, an eerie plopping sound.

Beneath them there were rows of vats sunk deep into the concrete floor. Darren's torch was the pound-shop variety, and didn't have enough power to illuminate the insides. He looked along the bridge to a set of metal steps that led to a glassed-in viewing room. 'Let's go,' he said. 'That's the way into the rest of the building.'

'What if the steps aren't safe?' whined Stuffy. 'This place has been empty a long time.'

'You're full of crap,' laughed Darren. 'Anything that's going to go in this building has already gone.' He jumped up and down to prove it. The walkway vibrated and hollow sounds rang out.

'Cut that out,' yelled Jake. He was having second thoughts too. 'What if the dog comes after us? That thing will be looking to get even.'

'I've got a stun gun,' said Darren. 'Not that I'll need it. The dog's a chicken. It ran right past me last night when I was down at the river. It's not the people-eating kind.' He walked as he talked, and they followed him through the viewing room and into a wide hall full of doorways. The torch was getting weary and both ends of the corridor stayed dark.

The harsh rip of wood being prised from nails interrupted the quiet. The sounds were outside, but they were close. There were voices too. Someone was trying to get in through the front door.

'Sounds like we've got competition,' said Darren. He turned to the others. There was no one there. Jake and Stuffy had run out on him.

At a room near the end of the hall, Cash listened to the sounds, the echoes, the voices, the rattle of doors and the scrape of heavy feet. It was almost train time. Silently she padded to the doorway. All her instincts told her to go down the hall and to her ramp. To get out. But there was someone in the hall blocking her exit.

She turned away and padded to the stairwell. She went up.

TWENTY-SEVEN

PC Dean came to the end of Chester Street and rolled down the window of his car. Miss Smithers was there, staring down the dark field.

'You're out late,' he said.

Miss Smithers turned around. 'I've been waiting for you,' she said simply. 'The dog's got to be in there.' She pointed to the distant distillery cutting a black hole in the night sky.

PC Dean didn't need an explanation. He and Sarah Smithers were on the same page. He got out of the car and reached for his binoculars. A tiny light flashed in one window of the distillery. The second time it flashed, Dean reached for his phone. 'I don't know about the dog,' he said. 'But something's in there all right.' He radioed in his position and turned back to the young woman next to him. There was starlight swimming in her violet eyes. 'It's been lovely talking to you, Miss Smithers,' he said. 'But I think you should go home now.'

PC Dean started into the field. He walked for about ten yards and then he broke into a jog.

Miss Smithers gave him a ten-second head start. Then she ran after him. She was fast and light. Like a cat. They reached the distillery in a dead heat.

O'Rourke was watching the local news in his living room. He was furious. Jane had laughed out loud when he'd popped the question. She'd told him she wasn't going to live in a pokey house by the river and be wifey number three, with or without the boy. He hauled himself from the couch unsteadily and grabbed his coat. He was sick of it all. He'd go down to the pub.

Mackenzie hadn't come home. The letter from Kid lay open on the table.

Mackenzie was watching the news on a TV in a shop window on the high street. He jammed his hands into his pockets. He'd spent a long cold day checking out the backs of the warehouses. He had walked the whole length of Chester Street too, eavesdropping on the reporters and the neighbours whenever he could get close enough. No one had seen the dog.

The television screen panned across the development field. Mackenzie felt a wave of heat when the distillery came into view. Cash was there. He just knew it.

He took off at a run.

TWENTY-EIGHT

Cash came out of the stairwell into a wide-open room on the top floor. The pitched roof was strapped with funnels and pipes and coils. Over the floor a maze of machines and vats set up an obstacle course. One side was all windows, tiny panes with wire mesh over them, many of them cracked or broken. The March moonshine streamed inside, and night breezes scraped over the shards of glass and whistled between the wire grids.

Silently Cash moved behind a cooker into the shadows, listening to the footsteps. She lowered her head. The hairs along her ruff came up. Her ears

155

went back. Growls caught in her throat as she moved deeper into the mess of machinery. In the centre of the room a giant funnel hung down from the steep roof. A guard rail curved around it, and Cash began to circle the room, following its circumference.

Darren left the stairwell cautiously. It was a bright night and the dust glistened. His torch died and he waited, letting his eyes adjust to the moonlight. White patches hovered above the floor.

Darren readied the stun gun. The dog was almost in the centre of the room and he hurried to keep the white patches in sight, scrambling over the railing and cutting across the space, closing the distance between them. He ducked to go under the funnel just as a wandering cloud cut across the moon and turned the room black. Darren stumbled.

The hole in the floor took him by surprise.

He dropped like a stone.

The old grain chute was greased with years of dust. Vainly Darren rammed both arms outwards against the slick metal sides, pushing with his palms, trying to slow his descent. The friction seared his skin and he began to scream. Then the chute angled and spat him into midair.

For a split second he flailed in space. It was just long enough for him to grasp where he was going. He managed to get in one short sweet breath before icy water closed over his head.

He sank.

The sounds of the splash echoed up the chute. Cash danced around the hole, angling her ear to hear better. Then she found her voice. At last. She barked out loud. She barked and barked some more. The noise of it raised the dust and set the machinery vibrating. The whole distillery rang out.

PC Dean wrestled a second board from the front entrance. 'Stay here,' he ordered before crawling through the opening.

Miss Smithers was right behind him.

They made for the stairwell and pounded upwards, following the direction of Cash's barks. Dean's police torch was powerful. When they reached the top, it lit up the whole room: the machines, the dust, the fence, the hole in the floor. Cash stood next to the hole staring back, her eyes glowing like amber flames. She had finished her barking. She had made up her mind.

She jumped.

They could hear her sliding down the chute, her claws scrabbling against the metal sides. A loud splash followed.

'The dog's slid right down to the cellar!' Dean declared. He turned to retrace his footsteps and Miss Smithers ran by his side. They got back to the front hall just as Mackenzie clambered through the gap in the front door.

'Miss Smithers!' he gasped as PC Dean and his teacher ran past. He raced behind them as they flashed through the glass viewing room onto the walkway, yelling out for his dog all the while. 'Cash! Cash! Where are you?'

Dean aimed his torch into the centre of the cavernous cellar. 'Cash!' Mackenzie yelled again. 'Cash, I'm coming! Where are you?' He strained to see into the cisterns set into the concrete floor.

Miss Smithers touched Mackenzie on the collar. 'Be quiet,' she urged. 'Listen!'

A long time ago the giant cisterns had been connected to the river, a series of cleaning tanks for the dregs of the whisky. When the building was condemned, the tanks had been sealed. They should have been empty. But water is patient. Over the years the river had found its way back. Now the cistern under the chute was four metres full of water. A light mist hovered over it. And something inside was panting for air.

'She's there,' yelled Mackenzie. He ran down the iron steps and led the others to the big bowl set into the floor. Dean directed his torch over the lip.

Three metres down, a dog struggled to stay on the surface of the water. In her powerful jaws she gripped a shirt collar. She was holding up a boy. The boy's eyes were closed. He was no more than a dead weight.

There was no way for the dog to get out. And there was no way for them to get down to help her, either.

The cold water and the struggle to hold up the unconscious boy were having their effect. The dog was moving with more effort, hopelessly, the cold numbing her body, her burden pulling her down. Her breathing sounded ragged, waterlogged.

'Cash,' yelled Mackenzie. 'Cash, hold on.'

PC Dean panned his torch over the cellar floor. An old metal ladder lay to the side of the cistern. It had a hook at the top and he dragged it over to the edge of the vat. When he tipped it inside, the hook grabbed the lip and the last rung of the ladder disappeared below the water line. 'This'll work,' he declared, stripping off his shoes and coat. He gave his torch to Miss Smithers. 'Point this at the dog.'

Then he began making his way down the rungs.

Cash was too tired to care. She didn't trust the man any more than she trusted Darren. Her mind was slipping into a place where it was dark and cold. But she had her instincts, and she wasn't letting go. She'd drown first.

Mackenzie leaned over. 'Cash!' he cried. 'Hold on, Cash. You can do it. Hold on, girl. You've got to.'

Miss Smithers grabbed on to him. 'You'll fall in too,' she said. 'The dog's got enough to do. Just keep talking. It's listening to you.'

She was right. The dog was swimming steadier now. She had heard the boy.

Her boy!

PC Dean reached the water and stuck out his free hand. The dog was too far away. 'Get that boy over by the ladder,' he yelled. 'The dog's listening to him.'

'Come over here,' Miss Smithers said gently to Mackenzie. 'The dog's got to let PC Dean have the young man. You've got to tell it what to do.'

Mackenzie leaned over the ladder. 'Cash, come here, girl,' he spoke firmly. Just like he used to, when he had to explain something to her. 'It's all right. Come!'

Cash responded. She began to paddle towards the light, towards PC Dean, with the last of her strength. The policeman reached out. He held on to the frozen ladder with one hand and grabbed Darren with the other. Moving quickly he somehow heaved the boy over his shoulder and started to climb.

It was rough going. The boy's body was as heavy as lead.

Mackenzie and Miss Smithers grabbed hold of Darren when PC Dean reached the top. They stretched his still form out on the concrete. The policeman crawled off the ladder and started to press on the boy's lungs. *Press. Release. Press. Release.* He squeezed out the stagnant river water.

Darren started to cough.

Mackenzie was already on the ladder, heading into the treacherous water. 'Hold on, Cash!' he cried. 'I'm coming.' Down he went, right to the water's edge and then beyond it to the last rung. He reached out to his dog, but Cash was past thinking. She was pawing the water frantically, choking. She was running on empty.

PC Dean started down the ladder to help. But Mackenzie was already doing what needed to be done. He yanked off his old belt and looped it into a collar. He hooked his legs into the rungs for grip and lunged for his dog. Throwing the noose around her neck, he dragged her close.

Now they were stuck against the ladder. Mackenzie didn't have enough strength to climb back up himself, let alone haul up a soaking wet pit bull too.

'Talk to her, Mackenzie,' said Miss Smithers firmly, leaning over the lip of the vat. 'Talk to your dog. You've got to give her hope.'

And so Mackenzie did. 'Cash. Cash, we've got to get up the ladder. Please, Cash. We've got to go up. Up, girl. Up!'

Cash focused. She tried to grab the rungs, her forepaws slipping on the metal. But her hind legs were too far under the water. She didn't have any way to push up. She was stuck. She was spent.

But she was a pit. She kept trying.

Mackenzie saw right away what had to be done.

He took a deep breath and lowered himself into the dark water, gripping the bars on the way down. The shock of the cold shoved the air right back out of his lungs. When his head went under, icy needles knifed his thinking. But he went down further, pushing his hands up against the last rung to stay submerged, down until he was right under his dog's hind legs. He rammed his shoulders up against her back paws.

Then he began to pull himself up.

Once Cash felt her boy under her back feet, she knew what to do. One front paw hooked around a higher rung. She started to climb.

Mackenzie cleared the water line and began to choke. He choked and shook. But he kept going up, coaxing the dog forward, pushing with his shoulders.

PC Dean climbed off the ladder and reached over the edge of the vat to grab Cash's neck. Miss Smithers grabbed PC Dean. And Mackenzie gave Cash's rump one last shove. She scrambled over the edge onto the concrete. And so did Mackenzie.

They all collapsed in a muddle.

Mackenzie hugged his dog. 'Cash,' he chattered. 'I'm so sorry. I love you, Cash.'

Cash reached out to give him a lick, a shaky

shivery ice-cream lick.

They could hear the police now, the back-up team, pouring into the building. PC Dean yelled out his location.

Miss Smithers reached over to Darren. He was still coughing, his eyes shut. When he finally opened them, he got a good eye-level look at Cash. He closed his eyes again quickly.

PC Dean stood back and let his colleagues do their job. He was shivering more than jelly on a dance floor. Miss Smithers had to hold him close to warm him up.

Soon there were blankets for everyone.

Darren was taken to the hospital.

Mackenzie was wrapped up and so was Cash. The two of them went home in a squad car. When they pulled up to Mackenzie's house, all the lights were on. Someone was standing at the front door.

'D'you know that boy?' said the officer in the police car.

'Yes,' said Mackenzie. 'That's Kid. He's my brother.'

Miss Smithers got all wrapped up in blankets too. PC Dean leaned into the back window of the squad car that was taking her home. 'Miss Smithers,' he asked. He was still shivering so he stuttered a bit. 'Wi-will you ma-marry me?'

She peered up at him through the window with those big violet eyes, and put out her hand. 'I can't get married,' she said. 'At least, not yet. I have things to do. But I'll ... I'll think about it ...'

Jimmy Cormorant snapped a picture of the two of them leaning in towards each other. 'Will you settle for an interview?' he asked.

TWENTY-NINE

PC Dean headed for the animal shelter first thing in the morning.

'How's my dog doing?' he asked. 'The pit bull that came in a few days ago.'

The girl at the front desk smiled. 'See for yourself,' she said. 'He's the only one we've got left now. It's a good thing you put your name down for him. It seems the pit bulls have made a comeback. Some mother with her little girl picked up a really friendly white bitch yesterday. It was the last one, except for yours.'

PC Dean went into the vet's rooms at the back. The

dog was rooting around in a blanket. He looked up at the man hopefully. His eye was still swollen, but most of his wounds were closed and the hair was beginning to grow back. He smelled of talcum powder.

'You're a sorry sight,' said PC Dean.

The dog began to wag his tail.

'How long before I can take him home?' said PC Dean to the girl.

'Now's as good a time as any,' said the girl. 'Vet's given the thumbs-up.'

Mackenzie and Cash woke up in a mess of blanket. They smelled musty, like old river water. Kid leaned down from the upstairs bunk.

'Time to get up, brother,' he laughed. 'It's moving day.'

'Where are we going?' said Mackenzie.

Kid got out of bed and sat on the bottom bunk. Cash had to shift to make room. Kid got serious. 'Had a talk with the old man,' he said. 'I've got a room in town. It's not fancy, but I reckon we'll get on all right. You'll have to change schools.'

'What about Cash?' Mackenzie rubbed the dog's head.

'That dog is part of the family. She's welcome.'

'What about Dad?'

Kid's face darkened. 'He's got to get himself sorted,' he said finally. 'So it's just you and me for now.'

In her living room, under a blanket, Miss Smithers was having her morning tea in front of the TV. Jimmy Cormorant was reporting the lead story.

'At noon today, Bylaw 132 receives final assent. From now on no pit bull in the Crickstead region can appear in public without a muzzle. Owners refusing to follow the law risk having their dog taken from them on the spot. All pit bulls without owners and all unborn shall be euthanized.'

There was a pause before Jimmy continued.

'But that, viewers, is not the end of our story. For it appears that the people in this city have opened their minds and their hearts. As of this morning at nine-thirty, no animal shelter in the area has any pit bull in residence. Every single pit bull has found a home. There will be no slaughter of the innocents today.'

Jimmy paused for effect. 'Some of the owners who adopted the last stragglers have agreed to say a few words on camera.'

Angus Smooth stood outside the pound. His dog was wearing a muzzle and looking ready to fight. 'My new dog and I are going for socialization,' he said. 'Classes start in the morning. Right now, all this dog knows how to do is fight, but those classes will teach it to love and pay attention. They'll be good for me too.' The man grinned. 'I gave up fighting six years ago.'

Another owner, an old lady this time, stroked her new dog. 'This is Annie,' she said. 'She's got a bad back and hardly any teeth. I should think we'll spend our last few years together taking it easy.'

A Chinese restaurant owner showed off his dog. 'A chow mein dog,' he said proudly. 'Eats tofu too.'

Jimmy came back on the screen to finish his report. 'Last night our Wonder Dog performed a final act of service. She hauled a drowning teenager out of an old vat in the derelict distillery at the Clover Cup development field. That near-tragedy has mobilized our city. Today word has it that the council and the developers have reached an agreement. The distillery will be restored as a historic site. The Clover Cup development is going ahead. And there will be a new community centre this time next year.'

The last shot showed Jimmy on the field beside the development sign. 'On a final note, *City News* is glad to tell its viewers that the mysterious dog that spoke to the hearts of the people is now reunited with her owner. So she too will be saved from the harsh sanctions of Bylaw 132.'

As the story switched to a report on traffic, the *City News*'s editor-in-chief called Jimmy. He was pleased. Ratings were up – way up. The editor promised his young reporter first crack next time a big story came in.

Darren took the six o'clock train out of town in the custody of his parents. He knew when he was beaten. The police had been clear about his choices: go home or be charged. Carrying a stun gun, dog fighting, trespassing … they seemed to have a long list. So Darren had no choice.

Neither did his parents.

Mrs Brody enjoyed the news on the TV. So did the old tom cat. They were curled up in their temporary accommodation while the insurance people fixed up Mrs Brody's house.

Mrs Brody put on her slippers. 'Let's heat up some milk in the microwave,' she said to the cat. She went into the kitchen and filled a cup and a saucer. 'I'll have to get one of these contraptions when we go back home.'

The old tom just rubbed up against her leg.

THIRTY

Mackenzie was sitting at the makeshift table. His brother was already at work. There was a note stuck to the old fridge. Mackenzie looked at it and grinned. It said more than usual.

Hey Mack,
I'm on the early shift at the hospital. There's someone I want you to meet. She'll be coming home with me after her check-up. You'll like her. Her name's Abi. She's dying to meet you and Cash. She says she's daft about dogs.

**Do me a favour and clean up the place!
Pick some dandelions or something.
Kid**

Outside the kitchen door, Cash snoozed on the fire escape, her nose wedged under the iron gate across the steps. The sun was ripe enough to set her coat glowing like corn oil. It was all she could do to open one eye. Behind her she could hear the crunch of bran flakes and the voices on the TV.

Cash wasn't interested in the news. She sniffed the air. The alley between the buildings had a curious mix of smells that morning – washing powder, orange peel, oil. From her perch she stared sleepily down to the narrow strip of street.

PC Dean was out walking. Saturdays were his day off. He had his dog on a lead. Both Cash's eyes snapped open when they strolled by. Her ears went up. She knew that dog.

PC Dean's dog was doing a high-stepping march down the street. His tail curved proudly over his back. A bright blue muzzle decorated his snout. The dog was proud of that muzzle. It was a present from the man – *his* man.

PC Dean was high-stepping too. He had a young woman on his arm. The woman turned and looked into the alley. Even from all that distance, Cash recognized those big eyes.

She wagged her tail a little.

'Cash.' Her boy came out on to the fire escape. 'Come on, Cash. Let's go for a walk. We've got to pick some flowers.'

Cash stood up and stretched. She stuck her snout into the boy's hand.

Mackenzie bent over to rub her ear. It crumpled like heavy silk. 'Aw, Cash,' he said. 'I love you, Cash.'